Praise for
Kristine Kathryn Rusch

"Rusch is a great storyteller."

—*RT Book Reviews*

"Whether [Rusch] writes high fantasy, horror, sf, or contemporary fantasy, I've always been fascinated by her ability to tell a story with that enviable gift of invisible prose. She's one of those very few writers whose style takes me right into the story—the words and pages disappear as the characters and their story swallows me whole….Rusch has style."

—Charles de Lint

"A masterful writer is at work."

—Orson Scott Card
New York Times bestselling author

"Rusch's greatest strength…is her ability to close down a story and leave the reader feeling that the author could not possibly have wrung any more satisfaction out of the piece."

—*The Kansas City Star*

"Rusch is a great storyteller—easily the equal of Patterson or Koontz."

—*Analog*

"Kristine Kathryn Rusch is one of the best writers in the field."

—*SFRevu*

"[Rusch's] writing style is simple but elegant, and her characterization excellent."

—Mark Morris
Beyond

"Like early Ray Bradbury, Rusch has the ability to switch on a universal dark."

—The *Times* of London

Praise for *The White Mists of Power*

"Moves at a whirlwind pace through political intrigue… A remarkable amount of plot as well as beguiling characters."

—*Publisher's Weekly*

"A prince reclaiming his lost kingdom is…a compelling story. Rusch provides some unusual twists. Every bit as good as her fine short fiction."

—*Science Fiction Chronicle*

"A traditional high fantasy novel…Rusch has added elements to make it original and unique. The story is strong, the magic subtle and mysterious."

—*Locus*

Also by
Kristine Kathryn Rusch

The Fey Series:

Destiny (A Short Novel)
Sacrifice
Changeling
The Rival
The Resistance
Victory
Black Queen
Black King

Standalone Fantasy Novels:

The White Mists of Power
Heart Readers
Traitors

Five Fantastic Tales
Kristine Kathryn Rusch

WMG
Publishing

Five Fantastic Tales

Second Edition
Copyright © 2012 Kristine Kathryn Rusch
Published 2012 by WMG Publishing
www.wmgpublishing.com
Cover art copyright © Andreus/Dreamstime
Book and cover design copyright © 2012
by WMG Publishing
Cover design by Allyson Longueira/WMG Publishing
ISBN-13: 978-0-615-73043-1
ISBN-10: 0-615-73043-4

"Flower Fairies" by Kristine Kathryn Rusch first published in *Realms of Fantasy*, October, 2009.

"The Poop Thief" by Kristine Kathryn Rusch first published in *Enchantment Place*, edited by Denise Little, Daw Books, 2008.

"Domestic Magic" by Kristine Kathryn Rusch first published in *Witch High*, edited by Denise Little, Daw Books, 2008.

"Say Hello To My Little Friend" by Kristine Kathryn Rusch first published in *Imaginary Friends*, edited by John Marco and Martin H. Greenberg, Daw Books, 2008.

"Victims" by Kristine Kathryn Rusch first published in *Sisters of the Night*, edited by Barbara Hambly and Martin H. Greenberg, Warner Aspect, 1995.

WMG Publishing
www.wmgpublishing.com

Contents

Five Fantastic Tales

Kristine Kathryn Rusch

Introduction

SOMETIMES I THINK I write fantastic stories because I can't see very well. My relationship with my eyes has always been iffy. Or perhaps it's best to say my relationship with my glasses.

I got glasses around the age of ten, but I needed them much earlier. I lied about it. I kept telling my parents my eyes were just fine. When they finally got my eyes tested, I needed pretty serious glasses. My mother, ever practical, bought the cheapest pair, some unfashionable cat's eyes with rhinestones.

I stepped on them the very next day *on purpose* and told Mother that some other kid (unnamed) had done it. I don't know if she believed me, since she knew I wanted the more fashionable (and expensive) granny glasses. Off we went to the eye doctor who replaced my lenses in those horrible cat eye frames.

I stepped on the frames the next day.

This time, my parents caved in and I got the granny glasses. I took them off once I got to school, however, and only put them on when I really needed to see the chalkboard.

I was thirteen when my best friend pulled me aside and said, "You know, you look worse when you squint than you do when you wear your glasses." I practiced in front of the mirror and discovered that lo and behold, she was right.

I wore my glasses from then on. Then, at sixteen, I got contact lenses, and could see all the time.

But my bratty history with glasses means that I spent most of my formative years looking at a fuzzy world. A world where things weren't quite what they appeared. A world where an amorphous green and brown blob might be a tree or it might be a man wearing a brown suit and a green hat.

Without my glasses, the world was full of possibilities. And danger.

I often write about sneaky magic, little magic, magic that seems less powerful than it is. I think that comes from the disappointment of discovering a tree when I expected a man. Or realizing that the scary ghost-like thing at the edge of the yard is actually a shirt drying on a clothesline.

This little collection is filled with stories about sideways, little, and sneaky magic. It starts with "Flower Fairies," which is a rare story in that I dreamed it before I wrote it. I actually saw that little flower fairy peering out of her bouquet in a dream, got up, and wrote down the opening image before I forgot it.

Next, "The Poop Thief," which I fortunately did *not* dream. "The Poop Thief" didn't come from anything visual. Instead, it came from an ad on the radio for a lawn cleanup service. I, of course, took it the wrong way.

I wrote "Domestic Magic" for an anthology Denise Little put together in the height of the Harry Potter craze. She wanted a story about magic and high school. I was trying to figure out a way to write about something that wasn't Potterish. Instead of dealing with the most magical kid in school, I dealt with the least.

"Say Hello To My Little Friend" is an imaginary friend story. I have many imaginary friends—that's why I write. So, for me, "imaginary" and "friend" in combination does *not* mean someone who does not exist. And if I say any more, I ruin the story for you. Enjoy the whimsy, because the final story in the book isn't whimsical at all.

When I wrote "Victims" in the late 1990s, vampires were not considered sexy or anywhere close to human. If anything, this story has become more relevant over time. In its day, it was so unusual that the initial editor commented on the strange point of view.

Now it belongs in a collection of urban fantasy, right alongside the flower fairies.

This is my second five-story collection. The stories unite around a genre or a theme or a topic. Sometimes you'll find duplications. Sometimes you won't. What you will find are stories that should be together at a cheaper price than you would get them if you bought them as individual e-books.

I hope you like these five fantastic tales. There are five more in the future, and five more after that. In the past twenty years, I seem to have written a lot of stories. And the wonderful changes to the publishing industry have allowed me to make them available to you.

Enjoy.

—Kristine Kathryn Rusch
Lincoln City, Oregon
July 7, 2010

Flower Fairies

SHE STANDS BEHIND the bouquet of flowers, her little face barely visible through the green fronds. Her skin is the color of loam, her eyes the faded green of underwater seaweed, and her lips the dusky rose of the tulips that hide her.

My heart pounds. I see her among all the bouquets set on the long white table, but my colleagues don't. They're moving flowers, checking tags, figuring out which bouquet goes into what memorial chapel.

We have four funerals this afternoon and two viewings tonight. The funeral home is large, modern, with several exits and entrances, so none of the groups will see each other. Their music shouldn't even overlap.

On days like today—a Saturday, shortly after the winter holidays—I employ nearly a dozen people, some of whom just stand by the doors and make sure the right family goes to the right memorial chapel.

It's all very delicate and very sad, and I try very hard to make sure that my employees seem sympathetic. After hundreds of funerals, however, many people lose sympathy. They recognize the patterns and realize some people are loved, some are hated, and some are simply forgotten.

And then there are the very old, whose friends and family have died long ago.

The very old touch me. I can easily see myself as part of their ranks, alone and forgotten. I want someone to honor me when I die, just as I'm sure they wanted someone to honor them.

So I do. For their funerals, I put on my best dress, and sit in the chapels myself. The ceremony is often elaborate, planned for friends and family who are now gone. When that happens, it's clear the person never expected to live so long. Often she (and it usually is a she) planned her ceremony with my father or my grandfather.

We keep amazing records. My family has planned funerals for this town for more than a century. If an historian comes into our little parlor and asks to see the records from a burial sixty years before, I can find it. I can tell who presided and who attended.

I can also tell what kind of floral arrangements decorated the memorial chapel.

Flowers have always been my specialty.

Perhaps that's why I notice the flower fairies long before anyone else does.

This little girl looks no more than three, but looks can be deceptive, particularly among flower fairies. Three is a problem. Three means I might have to return her to her family.

When she realizes that I see her, she smiles. Her eyes brighten to emerald and actually twinkle.

She touches the flowers in front of her. Ferns accent a mix of dusty rose and purplish blue tulips, with a single well placed lily in the center.

"I made this," she says in a decidedly childlike voice.

Everyone in the room turns. The silence, which was already heavy, turns oppressive.

She doesn't seem to notice. She's smiling at me. She is as young as I feared.

"Isn't it pretty?" she asks.

I turn to my assistant Diane. Diane's skin is normally the color of chalk, but it's gone even paler now.

"Call Roderick," I say.

Roderick is the only one of the flower fairies who uses modern technology. He burns through cell phones like smokers burn through matches. Fortunately, he's smart enough to keep the same number with each phone change.

Diane slips out of the room. Technology usually doesn't work well in the presence of the magical.

I smile at the little girl. "Your flowers are lovely."

"Thank you," she says primly. Then she waits. She wants me to ask what it is she's doing here or, worse, what she wants.

I never ask the flower fairies what they want. That's the wrong question. It's a question—particularly with a magical child—that could get the questioner in decades of trouble.

"Is this your first bouquet?" I ask, not really wanting to hear the answer.

She nods. "Can I stay?"

I don't dare say no to her. Saying no to an infant flower fairy is much more dangerous than saying no to an adult.

"You can stay," I say and try not to cringe.

***

I WAS LITTLE MORE than a babe myself when I first met the flower fairies. My parents owned a summer cabin near one of the mountain lakes. It was the only place I'd lived that didn't smell faintly of formaldehyde.

Instead, it smelled of the cool, clear lake water—and flowers.

Flowers. Flowers everywhere. My father believed that the cabin's previous owners had planted thousands of perennials, not listening to my mother when she would remark that many of the flowers that covered our property every year were annuals. Not only that, but they often bloomed at the same time—peonies and geraniums, roses and lilacs, asters and snowdrops. Seasons seemed to mean nothing on our land, something I didn't appreciate until much later.

I must have been six when I stumbled onto the clearing. In those days, children—even young children—were allowed to wander so long as they came back in time for supper. I wore a watch with large hands. I'd learned to tell time two years before, and I adhered to the schedule rigidly.

The schedule gave me freedom, which I desperately needed. When you grew up above a funeral home, you knew more about sadness, mourning, and death than you should have. The entire house had an oppressive air—one I accepted as normal until I grew old enough to visit my friends.

Sunlight filtered through the trees, burning off the last of the early morning fog. That fog made everything seem opaque—the trees, tall and strong with their green leaves; the shadows, deep and dark and somehow welcoming; and the flowers, which covered the meadow like grass.

The colors would have been overwhelming but for the fog: Blues and reds and pinks and so very much white that it looked less like an accent color and more like a deliberate shade.

I stepped from my path in the trees, expecting to walk on a carpet of flowers, because that was what they looked like, a carpet that led to another part of the woods.

But I sank into them. The ground where the flowers grew was lower than the ground in the forest. I walked in a sea of blooms, shoulder-high, and I felt like I had found heaven.

My watch stopped and I was late for lunch, forbidden to go off on my own again for a week. By the time I returned, the flowers were taller, and I didn't like walking inside of their stalks. The darkness with its intermittent rays of sunlight frightened me—and even then, I knew there was something wrong here, something not completely normal.

But I visited the clearing every summer. I learned to remove my watch before I stepped inside, because it stopped every single time I went into the clearing.

But I was never late to lunch again—the fairies saw to that. For such capricious little creatures, they have oddly tender hearts.

✳✳✳

WE HAVE SIX MEMORIAL CHAPELS—two large, three medium, and one small, so that the family doesn't notice that the deceased has few friends. This afternoon's funerals will take place in both large chapels as well as two of the medium chapels.

We'll have crowds.

But the little girl's flowers aren't going to any of those chapels. They're going to the small chapel, on the far side of the building.

At six tonight, we're holding a viewing.

I don't expect anyone to come.

The deceased is Helena Spenser, one of the very old. The obituary that ran in the paper this morning said she was one hundred and five, but the age was just an estimate. Like so many of her generation, she was born at home and no one ever issued a birth certificate.

And like so many women before her, Helena Spenser often lied about her age.

I met Helena a decade ago, when she made her funeral plans. She was formidable, a woman who still had vestiges of unusual height. She carried herself like a dancer, back straight, moving with fluid grace.

I even remember the outfit she wore—a black dress trimmed with red, and decorated with a single rose in the dress's lapel. Her hat, a cloche which matched the dress in design and trim, tilted rakishly on her thick silver hair.

My office was small then; I hadn't yet built the new Memorial Center. We sat in what had once been the servant's quarters in my family's oversized Victorian and, heads bowed, decided how Helena Spenser's friends and family would celebrate her long life upon this Earth.

Only this morning's obituary warned me that Helena Spenser's family had died sixty years before in a devastating fire. Her close friends—a group of widowed women who had raised hell and money for our little town—died nearly two decades ago.

She had acquaintances, but not the kind that most older folk had. She had never left the home she built after her husband and sons died, so she had no retirement center bridge partners, no orderlies who cajoled her to eat, no nursing home directors who felt it their duty to attend the funeral of one of the "members." She never went to church, so no minister would feel obligated to say a few words about her passing.

While she'd been spectacular in life—an actress who became a playwright, a self-made woman who had somehow survived the loss of everyone who mattered to her when she was still in her forties, the center of society into her seventies, and a philanthropist until the day she died—she kept to herself.

There was to be no ceremony. I remembered that much without even checking her file.

Such nonsense, she'd said when I broached the topic all those years ago. *Show the world I'm dead and then burn what's left.*

I hadn't known about the fire then. I hadn't known about it until this morning when I read about her.

I'd known the obituary was coming; I'd called the paper myself to make sure I didn't have to fund a notice of the viewing from Helena Spenser's account. But I hadn't expected the obituary to be so detailed and rich, nor had I expected Helena Spenser's life to be so fascinating.

Although I probably should have.

I had only met her the once, and she'd made quite an impression on me.

***

WE HAVE NO OTHER FLOWERS for Helena Spenser's viewing, and that angers me. This woman gave millions in charity, and no organization that benefited from her benevolence thought to send a single memorial.

Granted, most people send flowers to funerals and Helena is only having a viewing. And in the middle of this morning's obituary, the paper had highlighted a box of memorials where money could be sent in lieu of flowers.

I understand charitable donations. I usually encourage them. But someone should remember this woman as she leaves this life to go to the next. Someone should decorate her chapel, just for a little while.

Looks like that someone will have to be me.

Each funeral has excess flowers. The family takes the cards and the bouquets that they want—if any—and then one of my employees discreetly asks if the family minds donating the remaining flowers to lonely nursing home and hospital patients.

Of course the family doesn't mind. The family doesn't want to think about the flowers because that's just one more thing to worry about.

Besides, flowers die too—and that's an often too visual reminder of the fact that their loved one has just left the world.

So I will take some leftover flowers and decorate Helena's chapel.

It became Helena's chapel this morning, when we moved her body from the embalming chamber to the casket and then moved the casket to the front of the room. The casket is polished lavender—not quite the model she picked out (that one has been discontinued) but close enough.

She looks lovely inside of it, nestled on satin that matches her hair. We didn't have to put much make-up on her. She doesn't look that much different from the woman who visited me in my office all those years ago.

She's wearing a black suit with purple piping. The black sets off her hair, the purple accents the casket itself.

It's too bad no one will see this. Rarely has our staff made a corpse look so good.

I check on her before the first funeral. I put the guest book near the entrance, so people can sign in and leave if they want to. I place the placard announcing the visiting hours just outside the door.

Right now, Helena looks lonely in her small chapel, without flowers and without notes. The piped-in music, all 1920s jazz, sounds a little too jaunty for the occasion. But I didn't pick it. She did.

She had planned everything down to the last detail.

Except, of course, the effects of age and time.

***

By late afternoon, Roderick still hasn't arrived. I've had Diane page him three more times. I even sent one of the lowliest assistants to the edge of the clearing not far from the old Victorian. This assistant will stand near the old growth tree stumps that dot the back of my property, and call for Roderick.

Roderick never comes when he's paged like that. Instead, he finds me, wherever I am, and reminds me he's not a dog.

Of course, this time, the verbal page isn't working either.

I can't wait. I have to ready the chapel just in case someone shows up for Helena's viewing.

Gingerly, I carry the little girl's bouquet into the chapel. The vase is made of obsidian. I've never seen anything so beautifully carved.

The flower fairy sits on the edge of the vase, her feet dangling off the side. Her little fingers caress the ferns. Her emerald eyes twinkle.

"Will everyone like the flowers?" she asks.

I can't answer that question. If I say yes and no one does, then I have lied to a flower fairy, which puts me at their mercy. If I hedge and say, *I hope so*, then I am insulting the little being who created this arrangement, because I'm telling her in a sideways fashion that the flowers aren't good enough. If I say *I don't know,* I lose standing with the flower fairies.

Instead, I stop outside the chapel doors. I look down the private hallway and make sure we're alone.

"Are you sure you want to remain with the bouquet?" I ask.

She nods. She's tiny and delicate and amazingly beautiful. She looks like a flower herself.

"These flowers are for grieving," I say.

"I know," she says. "That's why there's a lily."

The funeral flower, apparently, for flower fairies as well as for humans.

"All right," I say, and with one hand, pull open the heavy oak door leading into the chapel.

No matter how gently we perfume the air, the scents of death and formaldehyde linger. The body in the coffin never looks real. I am always amazed at how many people say that the deceased looks so happy or so alive or so beautiful.

Helena does look beautiful—for a wax doll—but the vibrant demanding woman I met the day we planned this event was much more beautiful. Animation, personality, that spark of life—it can't be faked, not with make-up and reconstruction and excellent posing.

It can only be mimicked.

I expect the flower fairy to gasp or be shocked. But she rides on her vase like a soldier going to battle. She does look up front as we walk. A small frown crosses her little face.

"Pretty," she says, and points.

At first, I think she's pointing at Helena. Then I realize she's pointing at the coffin.

"I want the flowers there," she says, still pointing.

I follow the point as best I can. I swallow, trying to think of a tactful way to tell her the arrangement is too small for such a large empty space.

"Usually," I say, "something as pretty as your arrangement goes on the shelf just behind the coffin."

I indicate the shelf near the podium. Usually three of the loveliest arrangements go there. But a single arrangement, particularly one this beautiful, would look spectacular there as well.

"No," she says and moves her finger up and down imperiously. "There."

She means the closed half of the coffin. I suppress a sigh and silently wish for Roderick.

Of course, he doesn't come.

"The viewing doesn't start until six," I say. "It's four now."

I'm not sure she understands. I'm trying to tell her, in a roundabout way, that she'll be alone. I don't dare say that bluntly because I'm afraid she'll use her budding magic to force me to stay or to bring in my assistants.

Or worse, to bring in everyone from one of the near-by services.

"It's all right," she says.

And I hope it is.

"I have some errands," I say. "I'll be back before the viewing starts."

"I know," she says and settles behind the fronds.

***

FOR THE NEXT HOUR, I try not to think of her alone in there. She's young and if young fairies are anything like young humans, then she must be bored.

If she's bored, she'll either sleep or she'll cause trouble.

I'm hoping for sleep, but part of me expects the worst.

After I leave her, I text Roderick. A plume of smoke rises from my Blackberry, so I know the text has gone through. I set it on vibrate and put it in my pocket.

Then I go to the largest chapel, where the final funeral is just ending.

The funeral is for the mayor's mother-in-law. She was a difficult woman, who never had a kind word to say about anyone, her son-in-law in particular.

The large crowd isn't here for her. They're here to see and be seen. It's funeral as political event. The mayor will be running for governor next fall, and, unless something goes wrong, he'll win. Everyone wants to be his friend, in whatever way they can accomplish that.

His wife is the only one crying. She's not sobbing. Instead, her eyes are leaking. She keeps wiping the tears away as if they anger her.

They probably do. No one should cry for the woman in the casket. Even in death, she looks mean. Her mouth is pinched from smoking, her fleshy cheeks forming jowls that we couldn't erase with make-up. She died of a massive heart attack while berating the head of the town council and the joke around town (spoken quietly and away from the mayor's hearing) that she had done the impossible: having a heart attack without having a heart.

The mayor is saying a few words. They're deft—he is truly a politician—and then he'll invite everyone forward to pay their last respects.

He has promised me all of the flowers—his wife wants none of them. I slip away, leaving the remainder of the ceremony to my able assistants, who can better stomach hypocrisy than I can.

Instead, I head back to my office, checking my Blackberry as I go.

It's not like the flower fairies to leave one of their children alone for so long. It's not like Roderick to ignore my pleas for assistance.

We've known each other since my days in the woods, back when I was a child. Roderick took care of me and his price (fairies always have a price) was to learn how to use modern technology.

Roderick wanted to cross between his world and ours. Mostly he manages it. People do notice him, but they think it's because they find him attractive. Somehow they miss the glamour that slides off him like glitter.

I'm about to text him again, when Diane catches my arm. I didn't even see her approach.

"You need to come with me," she says.

She was assigned to our other large funeral of the day, but that ended hours ago. I expect her to lead me to the big chapel. Instead, she takes me to the smallest chapel and carefully pulls open the door.

"Look," she says.

I'm afraid to. A magical child left alone in a place of the dead. I thought I was making a mistake. Now I will see exactly what that mistake is.

I peer inside, carefully, so that the girl can't see me.

My breath catches.

Flowers cascade off the closed casket. Lavender and bluebells mix with a carpet of greenery. The greenery outlines the aisle that flows all the way to the main door.

I remain in the hall and let the door close.

The child was bored, and she found a way to amuse herself. My heart catches.

"You didn't hear from Roderick, did you?" I ask Diane.

Diane shakes her head.

"I didn't notice," I say. "The flowers aren't covering Helena, are they?"

"I didn't notice either," Diane whispers.

We should check. One of us should go inside and make sure the girl didn't cover our corpse with a carpet of roses.

But I can't bring myself to send Diane in there, and I'm not going to go myself. I don't know how to tell a magical child—a flower fairy—to stop doing something.

I've been chastised by the flower fairies before.

I brought my father to their clearing, hoping he would ask them to do the flowers for his funeral home. They humored him, then made him forget.

And they punished me for sharing our relationship.

They made me promise that I would display any flowers they gave me, even when I became director of the family funeral parlor.

I agreed. I thought I had outsmarted them because I never planned to work with my family.

I was twelve.

I didn't understand the ways of the world.

I still honor that agreement, even though the contract has expired.

I have seen what happens when someone crosses them.

I adjust the placard on its board. Then I text Roderick again.

Urgent, I type. *Please. Help.*

The smoke rises, acrid and dark. He's getting my messages.

He's just not answering.

And I don't know why.

***

AT QUARTER TO SIX, I slip into the private bath behind my office and change into my best dress. This dress
is new; I bought it the day I heard of Helena's death. The
dress is black with red trim—not as glamorous as hers
was, but I can never do glamorous.

I don't wear a hat because hats indoors, particularly
at a funeral, are often considered bad luck. But I pile my
hair on top of my head and secure it. Then I slip one of
the hothouse roses—also red—into the makeshift bun.

I can never be as dramatically beautiful as Helena,
but I can at least honor her by looking my best.

I slip on a pair of black pumps and grab a glittery
black clutch purse.

Then I head for the smallest chapel.

Diane stands outside the door to usher in anyone
who shows up. It's a little after six. So far she's ushered in
no one. We've received no calls, no condolences, and no
questions about where to send cards.

Roderick hasn't come either.

I twist my fingers together. The little flower fairy
won't know that anything is amiss at the viewing, but
what do I do with her afterwards? I'm not sure she
should stay with the bouquet.

Diane grimaces at me as I approach. I recognize the
look; she hates these lonely viewings as much as I do.
We've done too many of them over the years.

"Want me to go in with you?" she asks.

I shake my head. "Send Roderick in, though, if he ever shows up."

She nods.

I grab the oak handle on the door and pull it open.

This time, my gasp is audible. Diane crowds beside me and gasps as well.

The chapel is covered in greenery. The pews are covered in a carpet of wildflowers, the floor itself looks like it's made of moss, and trees grow in the corners. Flowers bloom on the shelves—more roses than I've ever seen, carnations, and lilies in stunning displays.

But the bouquet on the casket remains, and so does the open part of the casket itself. Helena Spenser looks like she's resting on a bier made of flowers.

"My God," Diane breathes. Then she touches my arm. "If anyone shows, should I send them in?"

"Yeah," I say. I have no idea how I'll explain this, although I've had a few fairy-sponsored magical moments before, and I've found that simple works best. "If they ask, just tell them she loved flowers."

"Okay." Diane seems reluctant to move.

I know I am. But I've come to pay my respects, and I'm going to do that. Then I'm going to sit as if I'm family and watch over her until viewing hours end.

I step inside. The aisle is so soft that my heels pierce it. I wobble. I'll do damage as I walk, so I pull off the shoes and set them by the door. They're instantly covered with grass and purple crocuses. I wonder if I'll ever get them back.

I walk on the moss. It feels warm as sunlit ground. It's comfortable and soothing, like going barefoot in the glade.

Still, I step carefully. I'm not sure where the child is. I don't want to hurt her.

I walk up to the coffin. Helena's eyes are closed, her lashes brushing her heavily made up cheeks. She looks content, even though I'm not sure how. Corpses don't show emotion.

I glance at the bouquet, wondering how that infant fairy managed so much work in such a short period of time.

But I don't see her.

I tell myself this isn't unusual; to create this magical wonderland, she probably has to move around a lot.

But my heart is pounding.

What happens if I lost her?

What happens if she gets hurt?

I don't even know what to call her. Fairies guard their names jealously and they don't like pet names.

I decide to cajole her. "This room has never looked lovelier."

"Good." The voice behind me is male and it makes me jump.

I turn. The man behind me is taller than I am. He is so thin that my hand could probably encompass his waist. He wears leaves over his hips and down his legs, but his chest is bare.

His skin is green, his hair brown. Instead of looking strange, he looks gorgeous.

Such is the way of flower fairies.

"We have worked hard this afternoon," he says.

As he speaks, more fairies come out of the greenery. They're all heights, and thin. Some have green skin, some have loam-colored skin like the little fairy. Some have skin the color of ivory. Their hair often matches the flowers they carry. They are all barefoot. The men wear leaves like this man does, and the women wear skimpy dresses made of petals.

Since fairies wear nothing in the wild, they are covering themselves according to human custom.

"This is stunning," I say. "And quite unexpected."

The door in the back opens, and Roderick slips in. He's wearing a suit and it looks stranger than anything the other fairies wear. Normally, Roderick wears tight black jeans, a t-shirt with some Goth band I don't recognize, and heavy boots.

The suit looks like an Armani, perfectly tailored to his slender frame. The white shirt beneath accents the darkness of his skin. His normally spiky hair has been combed back, and his piercings are empty.

He looks like a teenage boy told to clean up for his grandmother's funeral.

"There you are," I say with so much relief it even surprises me.

He smiles. I thread my way through the throng of fairies and stop beside him.

"I tried to contact you," I say. "I was worried."

"It's a small price to pay," he says, then sweeps his hand toward the chapel.

As he does, I see the glamour fall from his arm. The scents of moss and sunlight and a hundred flowers follow that glamour.

"If I had warned you," he says, "this would not have happened."

"Why not?" I ask.

"Because this is your domain." He bows his head slightly. "We have invaded. We beg pardon."

He thinks they've done something wrong.

"Pardon granted," I say, because you never cross fairies, no matter how well you think you know them. "I appreciate the respect for my domain. But you do need to know that I would have allowed this."

He looks at me in surprise. So do some of the others.

"This is a non-denominational chapel," I say. "What that means is the family and friends can design the service they want for the deceased. Just as you have here."

The little girl climbs into his arm. She puts her thumb in her mouth and rests her head on his shoulder. She's watching me with those emerald eyes.

The fairies had sent her ahead because they knew I wouldn't object to her. They had tried to outthink me.

He cradles her close. "You would have allowed this?"

I nod. "It's lovely. I'm sure Helena would have appreciated it."

He says, "We wanted to honor her."

"She meant a lot to you," I say, falling into my role as funeral director.

"To all of us." He smoothes the little girl's hair. "We honor her, because she honored us."

I'm surprised. I thought my staff and I were the only ones who knew about the flower fairies.

"She saw you then," I say.

"Not at first." He rests his head on the little girl's for just a brief instant. "But every day for the last sixty years, she stopped and admired our flowers."

Sixty years. Since her family died.

"Then she would murmur how lovely they were. Gradually we revealed ourselves. She visited our flowers. She played with our children. She was a bright, warm spot in the middle of our day."

I thought of that for a moment. A woman who had lost her husband and children. A woman who was looking for a way to go on. She had found it in flowers each and every day.

Then she learned the secret behind the flowers and instead of being afraid, she embraced it.

She embraced them.

As I have never dared to do.

"Do you mind if I sit?" I ask.

"Is that what you planned to do?" he asks.

I nod.

"Do you do that at all such occasions?"

"No," I say. "Only the special ones."

And this one is very, very special.

"Let's all sit," he says. He leads me to the front pew, then joins me. The little girl has fallen asleep in his arms. She has his look around the eyes and lips. I wonder if she's his.

I know so little about him—about any of them—and I am afraid to ask.

One by one, they approach the open casket, and one by one, they drop a flower inside. The flower varies—sometimes it's a daffodil, sometimes an orchid. But it's always lovely and it always fits.

When they're done, they sit in the pews. Vines cover them. Honeysuckle grows along the walls. Wisteria covers the doors.

We bow our heads in silence to this great woman. We mourn her passing and we celebrate her life.

Then, when the viewing hours are over, they all stand—and vanish.

Except for Roderick. He remains beside me.

"We'll clean this up," he says.

"Leave it," I say. "We won't use the chapel for another two days."

He smiles and touches my face. "Come see us in the glade," he says. "We miss you."

Then he too vanishes.

I stare at the motes of glamour, still floating where he had been. Before, I would have heard a threat in his words.

I would have been frightened.

Fairies can be terrifying.

But it took Helena to remind me that they are also extremely special.

They honored me today by respecting my chapel while honoring her.

If I treat them kindly, perhaps one day, they will decorate my chapel and sit in silent vigil after I am gone.

I hope so. Because from now on, I will remember that while flower fairies are capricious, they have oddly tender hearts.

The Poop Thief

O KAY, THIS IS JUST WEIRD."

The voice came from the back of the store. It belonged to my Tuesday/Thursday assistant, Carmen. High school student, daughter of two mages, Carmen had no real talent herself, but she was earnest, and she loved creatures, and I loved her enthusiasm.

"I mean it, Miss Meadows, this is weird."

Oddly enough, weird is not a word people often use in Enchantment Place. Employees expect weird. Customers demand it. What's weird here is normal everywhere else—or so I thought until that Tuesday in late May.

"Miss Meadows...."

"Hold on, Carmen," I said. "I'm with a client."

The client was a repeat whom I did not like. I'm duty bound at Familiar Faces to provide mages with the proper familiars—the ones that will help them augment their talents and help them remain on the right path (doing no harm, avoiding evil, remaining true to the cause, all that crap). I do my best, but some people try my patience.

People like Zhakeline Jones. She was a zaftig woman who wore flowing green scarves, carried a cigarette in a cigarette holder, and called everyone "darling." Even me.

I called her Jackie, and ignored the "It's Zhakeline, dahling." Actually, it was Jacqueline back when we were in high school and then only from the teachers. The rest of us called her Jackie, and her friends—what few she had—called her Jack.

Whenever she came in, I cringed. I knew the store would smell like cigarettes and Emerude perfume for days afterwards. I didn't let her smoke in here—Enchantment Place, for all its oddities, was regulated by the City of Chicago and the City of Chicago had banned smoking in all public places—but that didn't stop the smell from radiating off her.

Most of my creatures vacated the front of the store when she arrived. Only the lioness remained at my feet, curled around my ankles as if I were a tree and Zhakeline was her prey. A few of the mice looked down on Zhakeline from a shelf (sitting next to the books on specialty cheeses that I'd ordered just for them), and a couple of the birds sat like fat and sassy gargoyles in the room's corners.

Nothing wanted to go home with Zhakeline, and I didn't blame them. She'd brought back the last three familiars because the creatures had the audacity to sneeze when they entered her house (and silly me, I had thought that cobras couldn't sneeze, but apparently they do—especially when they don't want to stay in a place where the air is purple). We were going to have to find her something appropriate and tolerant, something I was beginning to believe impossible to do.

On the wall beside me, lights shimmered from all over the spectrum, then Carmen appeared. Actually, she'd stepped through the portal from the back room to the shop's front, but I'd specifically designed the magical effect to impress the civilians.

Sometimes it impressed me.

Carmen was a slender girl who hadn't yet grown into her looks. One day, her dramatic bone structure would accent her African heritage. But right now, it made her look like someone had glued an adult's cheekbones onto a child's face.

"Miss Meadows, really, my parents say you shouldn't ignore a magical problem and I think this is a magical problem, even though I don't know for sure, but I'm pretty certain, and I'm sorry to bother you, but jeez, I think you have to look at this."

All spoken in a breathless rush, with her gaze on Zhakeline instead of on me.

Zhakeline smiled sympathetically and waved a hand in dismissal. Bangles that had been stuck to her skin loosened and clanked discordantly.

"This hasn't really been working, Portia." Zhakeline said with a tilt of the head. She probably meant that as sympathy too. "I've been thinking of going to that London store—what do they call it?"

"The Olde Familiar." I spoke with enough sarcasm to sound disapproving. Actually, my heart was pounding. I would love it if Zhakeline went elsewhere. Then the unhappy familiar—whoever the poor creature might be—wouldn't be my responsibility.

"Yes, the Olde Familiar." She smiled and put that cigarette holder between her teeth. She bit the damn thing like a feral F.D.R. "I think that would be best, don't you?"

I couldn't say yes, because I wasn't supposed to turn down mage business and I could get reported. But I didn't want to say no because I would love to lose Zhakeline's business.

So I said, "You might try that store in Johannesburg too, Unfamiliar Familiars. You can see all kinds of exotics. But remember, importing can be a problem."

"I'm sure you'll help with that," she said.

"Legally I can't. But you're always welcome here if their wares don't work out."

The mice chittered above me, probably at the word "wares." They weren't wares and they weren't animals. They were sentient beings with magic of their own, subject only to the whims of the magical gods when it came to pairings.

The whims of the magical gods and Zhakeline's eccentricities.

"I'll do that," she said. Then she turned to Carmen. "I hope you settle your weirdness, darling. And for the record, your parents *are* right. The sooner you focus on a magical problem, the less trouble it can be."

With that, she swept out of the store. Two chimpanzees crawled through the cat doors on either side of the portal holding identical cans of Febreze.

"No," I said. "The last time you did that we had to vacate the premises. Or don't you remember?"

They sighed in unison and vanished into the back. I didn't blame them. The smell was awful. But Febreze interacted with the Emerude, leading me to believe that what Zhakeline wore wasn't the stuff sold over the counter, but something she mixed on her own.

Without a familiar, which was probably why the stupid stuff lingered for days.

"Miss Meadows." Carmen tugged on my sleeve. "Please?"

I waved an arm so that the store fans turned on high. I also uttered an incantation for fresh ocean breezes. (I'd learned not to ask for wind off Lake Michigan; that nearly chilled us out of the store one afternoon). Then I followed Carmen into the back.

Walking through the portal is a bit disconcerting, especially the first time you do it. You are walking into another dimension. I explain to civilian friends that the back room is my Tardis. Those friends who don't watch *Doctor Who* look at me like I'm crazy; the rest laugh and nod.

My back room should be a windowless 10x20 storage area. Instead, it's the size of Madison Square Garden. Or two Madison Square Gardens. Or three, depending on what I need.

Most of my wanna-be familiars live here, most of them in their own personal habitats. The habitats have a maximum requirement, all mandated by the mage gods and tailored to a particular species. Each bee has a football-sized habitat; each tiger has about a half an acre. Most creatures may not be housed with others of their kind, unless they're a socially needy type like herding dogs or alpha male cats. The creatures have to learn how to live with their mage counterparts—not always an easy thing to do—and its best not to let them interact too much with other members of their species.

Theoretically, I get the creatures after they complete five years of familiar training (and yes, you're right; very few familiars live their normal lifespan. Insects get what to them seems like millions of years and dogs get an extra two decades; only elephants, parrots, and a few other exceptionally long-lived species live a normal span).

That day, I had too many monkeys of various varieties, one parrot return who'd managed to learn every foul word in every language known to man (and I mean that) during his aborted tenure with his new owner, several large predatory cats, twenty-seven butterflies, five gazelle, sixteen North American deer, eight white wolves, one black bear, one grizzly return, one-hundred domestic cats, five-hundred-sixty-five dogs, and dozens of other creatures I generally forgot when I made a mental list.

Not every animal was for sale. Some were flawed returns—meaning they couldn't remember spells or they misquoted incantations or they weren't temperamentally suited to such a high-stress job. Some were whim returns, brought back by the mage who either bought on a whim or returned on a whim. And the rest were protest returns. These creatures left their mage in protest, either of their treatment or their living conditions.

All three of Zhakeline's returns had been protest returns although she tried to pass the first off as a flaw return and the other two as whim returns. It gets hard for a mage after a few rejections. Eventually she gets a reputation as a familiarly challenged individual, and might never get a magical companion.

And if she goes without for too long, she'll have her powers suspended until she goes through some kind of rehab.

Fortunately, that's never my decision. I'd seen too many mages fight to save their powers just before a suspension: I never want all that angry magic directed at me.

Carmen was standing on the edge of the habitats. They extended as far as the eye could see. My high school assistants didn't tend the habitats the way that civilian high school assistants would tend cages at, say, a vet's office. Instead, they made sure that the attendants that I hired from various parts of the globe (at great expense) actually did their jobs.

Each attendant had to log in stats: food consumed, creature health readings, and how often each habitat was entered, inspected, and cleaned. Then they'd log in the video footage for the past day—after inspecting it, of course, for magical incursions, failed spells, or escape attempts.

Carmen had called up our stats on the clear computer screen I'd overlaid over the habitat viewing area. She zoomed in on one stat—product for resale.

I frowned at the numbers. They were broken down by category. The whim returns and most of the protest returns were listed, of course, along with byproduct—

methane from the cows (to be used in various potions); shed peacock feathers (for quills); and honey from the bees that had convinced the mage gods to make them hive familiars, not individual familiars.

Those bees only went to special clients—those who could prove they weren't allergic and who could handle several personality types all speaking through their fearless leader, the sluggish queen.

"See?" Carmen asked, waving a hand at the numbers. "This week's just weird."

I didn't see. But I didn't have as much experience with the numbers as she did. And, truth be told, I didn't think her powers were in spell-casting. I believed they were in numerology—not as powerful a magic, but a useful one.

"I'm sorry," I said, feeling dense, like I often did when staring at rows of facts and figures. "What am I supposed to see?"

She poked her finger at one of the columns. The lighted numbers vanished, then reappeared in red.

"Available fertilizer," she said. "See?"

I stared at the category. Available Fertilizer. Our biggest seller because we undercut the competition, mostly so we could get rid of the crap quickly and easily.

"There's no number there," I said.

"Zero is a number," Carmen said with dripping disdain that only a teenager could muster.

"E…yeah…okay." I knew I was stammering, but the big honking nothingness made no sense. "The assistants haven't been cleaning the habitats?"

She pressed the screen, drawing down the earlier statistics. Cleanings had gone on as usual.

"So what happened to the fertilizer?"

"I have no idea where the fertilizer went," she said. "I'm not even sure it came out of the cages. I mean, habitats."

I had planned to give her a tour of the back, but I hadn't yet. So she always made the "cages/habitat" mistake, something she'd never say if she actually saw the piece of the Serengeti plain that Fiona, the lioness who liked to sleep under my cash register and Roy, the lion who supposedly headed her pride, had conjured up to remind themselves of home.

Cleaning the habitats was a major job, especially for the larger animals, and usually required extra labor. Entire families came in for an hour or two a night to clean grizzly's mountainside, especially during blackberry season.

I moved Carmen aside, pressed some keys only visible to me, and looked at several of the previous day's vids in fast motion. Habitat cleaning happened in all of them.

Habitat cleaners weren't required to log in what they cleaned unless the item was marketable which poop generally was. Animal poop that is. There's never a big market for insect poop.

Animal poop (ground up into a product called Familiar Fertilizer) had a wide variety of uses. Mages bought it for their herb gardens. In addition to being the Miracle Grow of the magical world, it also made sure that wolf's bane and all the other herbal ingredients of a really good potion, magical spell, or "natural" remedy was extra-powerful. Some mages vowed that anything fertilized with familiar poop could be safely sold with a money-back guarantee—especially (oddly enough) love spells.

"Must be a computer glitch," I said and stabbed a few more buttons.

"Let me." Carmen got to the correct screens quicker, without me even asking. She knew I wanted to check all that basic stuff—how many pounds of poop got ground into fertilizer at the nearby processing plant, how many pounds of fertilizer got shipped, and how many of our magical feed-and-seed brethren paid for shipments that arrived this week.

Each category had a big fat zero in the poundage column.

"I don't like this," I said. "You just noticed this?"

I tried to keep the accusation out of my voice. It wasn't her job to keep track of my shipments and my various product lines. She was a high school student working two days a week part-time after school.

I was the person in charge.

"I was going over the manifests like you taught," she said. "I let you know the minute I saw it."

Which was—I checked the digital readout on the see-through computer screen—half an hour ago, one hour after Carmen arrived.

Pretty dang fast, considering.

"I mean, everything was fine on Thursday."

Thursday. The last day she worked.

My lunch—an indulgent slice of Chicago pan-style

pizza—turned into a gelatinous ball in my stomach. "Can you quickly check the previous four days?"

"Already on it." She pressed a few keys.

I watched numbers flash in front of my eyes—too quickly for my number-challenged brain to follow. I could have spelled the whole thing, looked for patterns, but I had Carmen. She was better than any magical incantation.

"Wow," she said after a few minutes. "Those animals haven't pooped since Friday."

The gelatinous ball became concrete. I reached for the screen to look at health history, then stopped. A few of those creatures would have died if they hadn't pooped in three days. Some internal systems were less efficiently designed than others.

Still, I had her double-check the health records just to make sure.

"Okay," she said after looking at health records from Thursday to Tuesday. "So they all have normal bowel readings. What does this mean?"

"It means that your parents are right," I said.

"Huh?" She looked at me sideways, all teenager again. She hated hearing that Mom and Dad were right.

"Magical problems become bigger when they are allowed to fester."

"This is a magical problem?" she asked.

"The worst," I said.

She continued to stare at me in confusion, so I clarified.

"We have a poop thief."

***

YOU FIND POOP THIEVES throughout magical literature. Heck, you even find them in fairy tales.

Of course, they're never called poop thieves. They're "tricksters" who steal their victims' "essence." They're evil wizards who rob their enemies of their "life force."

Most scholars believe that these references are to sperm, which simply tells me that magical scholarship has been dominated too long by males. (Those inept male scholars don't seem to be able to read either; a lot of the victims are women who are, of course, spermless creatures one and all.)

The scholars are right in that "life force" and "essence" are often composed of bodily fluids. Some (female) scholars have assumed that this essence is blood, but blood is a lot harder to obtain than the simplest of bodily fluids—pee.

Pee, though, is like all other water. It seeps into the ground. It's difficult to get unless someone pees into a cup or a bottle or a box. (Or unless you've magicked the chamberpot—and there are a few of those stories as well [Those Brothers Grimm didn't like the chamberpot stories, and so kept them out of the official compilation.])

Poop, on the other hand…

Poop, actually, on either hand is a lot easier to obtain.

Poop, like pee, blood, and yes, sperm, is a life essence. Even in its nonmagical form it has magical powers. It gets discarded only to be spread on a fallow field. The nutrients in the waste material break down, enriching the soil which is often used to grow plants—plants which later become food. The food nourishes the person who eats it. The person's body processes the food into energy and vitamins and all sorts of other good stuff, and the leftovers become waste yet again.

Most of the non-magical have no idea the power held in a single turd.

Hell, most of the magical didn't either.

But the ones who did, well, they were all damn dangerous.

And I'd already lost too much time.

***

IT SEEMED ODD to call Mall Security at a time like this, but that was the first thing I did. Mine wasn't the only store with magical creatures.

If someone was stealing from me, then maybe he was stealing from the pet store down the way, the organ grinder monkey show just outside the food court, and the various holiday setups with their real Easter bunnies and Christmas reindeer and Halloween bats. Not to mention all the working familiars accompanying every single mage who walked into the place.

I let Carmen talk to Security. She was young enough and naïve enough to think they were sexy. She had no idea that most of them were failed magical enforcers or inept warlocks who'd been demoted from city-wide security patrol to Enchantment Place.

I stayed in the back room, bending a few rules because this was an emergency. Anyone who took that much poop had a plan. A big plan—or a need for a lot of power.

At first, I figured this thief simply wanted the magical support of a familiar without actually getting a familiar. Magical crime blotters were full of minor poop thieves who stole rather than get a new familiar of their own. They'd mine someone else's familiar, using the poop as a tool with which to obtain the magic, and no one would notice until that familiar got sick from putting out too much magical energy.

Maybe what we had here was a more sophisticated version of the neighborhood poop snatcher.

Which made Zhakeline a prime suspect.

But Zhakeline's magic had always been shaky at best, even when she had a familiar. That was why she looked so exotic and had so many affectations.

She had to appeal to the civilians who think we're all weird. She mostly sold her small magic services to them. If she predicted the future and was wrong or if she made a love potion that didn't work, the civilian would simply shrug and think to himself *Ah, well, magic doesn't really work after all.*

But the magical, we know when someone can't perform all of the spells in the year-one playbook. Zhakeline barely passed year one (charity on the part of the instructor) and shouldn't have passed from that point on. But that happened during the years when telling a kid that she had failed was tantamount to murdering her (or so the parents thought) and Zhakeline got pushed from instructor to instructor without learning anything.

Which was one of the many reasons I didn't want to give her another familiar.

And that was beside the point.

The point was that Zhakeline, and mages like her—the ones who needed the magical power of familiar poop—didn't have the ability to conduct a theft on this massive scale, at least not alone.

And even if they tried, they'd be better off going to the back yard of a mage with a canine familiar. There was always a constant poop supply, and it provided enough power—consistent power (from the same source)—so that the thief might become a slightly less inept mage, for a while, anyway.

Next I investigated my assistants. Most had no magical powers of their own, but had come from magical families. They knew that magic existed—and not in that hopeful *I wish it were so* way that a civilian had, but in a *this is a business* way that led them to peripheral jobs in the magical field.

They worked hard, most had a love of animals, insects or reptiles, and they often had a specialty—whether it was cooking the right kind of pet food or calming a petulant hyena.

I couldn't believe any of the assistants would be doing something like this because they would have to be working for someone else.

The nonmagical don't gain magic just by wishing on a powerful piece of poop.

I scanned records and employment histories. I scanned bank accounts (yes, that's illegal, but remember—emergency. A few rules needed to be bent), cash stashes and (embarrassingly) the last 48 hours of their lives. (Which, viewed at the speed of an hour per every ten seconds, looked like silent movies watched at double fast-forward.)

I saw nothing suspicious. And believe me, I knew what to look for.

Although I wished I didn't.

***

YOU SEE, I GOT THIS JOB, not because I have a particular affinity with animals or I'm altruistic and love pairing the right mage with the right familiar.

I got it because I have experience.

I know how to look for mages heading dark or mages who should retire or mages who mistreat their magic (and hence their familiars). I know how to take care of these mages quietly, efficiently, and with a minimum of fuss.

It didn't used to be this way. In the past, places like Familiar Faces existed on side streets and had just a handful of creatures, few of them exotic. Only in the last few years have the mega stores come into existence at high-end malls like Enchantment Place.

And even though we're supervised by the rules of the mage gods like all other familiar stores, we're run and subsidized by Homeland Security—Magical Branch.

(Not everyone knows there's a Homeland Security—Magical Branch, including the so-called "head" of Homeland Security. Hell, I even doubt the president knows. Why tell the person who's going to be out in four or eight years one of the world's most important secrets. Knowing this crew, they'd probably try to co-opt the Magical Branch into something dark. Better to keep quiet and protect us all.

(Which I do. Most of the time.)

My job here is to watch for exactly this kind of incursion. Technically, I'm supposed to report it, and then wait for the guys with badges to show up.

But I didn't wait for the guys with badges. I doubted we would have time.

(And, truth be told, I did want the glory. I was demoted to this position [you guessed that already, right?] for asking too many questions and for the classic corporate mistake, proving that the boss was an idiot in front of his employees. I'm a government employee and as such can't be fired without lots and lots of red tape [even in the magical world], so I was sent here, to Chicago where I grew up, to Enchantment Place where I have to put up with the likes of Zhakeline with a smile and a shrug and a rather pointed [and sometimes magically directed] suggestion.)

I toyed with rewinding time in all of the habitats—another no-no, but it would have been protected under the Patriot Act, like most no-nos these days. But rewinding time takes time, time I didn't really want to waste looking at creatures moping in their personal space.

Instead, I did some old-fashioned police work.

I went back out front where Carmen was still flirting with some generic security guard (and the mice were leaning over so far to watch that I was afraid one of them would fall down the poor man's ill-fitting shirt) and beckoned the lioness, Fiona.

She frowned at me, then rose slowly, stretched in that boneless way common to all cats, and padded through the portal ahead of me.

When I got back to the back, she was sitting on her haunches and cleaning her ears, as if she had meant to join me all along.

"We have a poop thief," I said, "and I think you know who it is."

She methodically washed her left ear, then she started to lick her left paw in preparation for cleaning her right ear.

"Fiona," I said, "if I don't solve this, something bad will happen. You might not get a home of any kind and none of the other familiars will be of use to anyone. You might all have to be put down."

I usually don't use euphemisms, and Fiona knew it. But she didn't know the reason that I used it this time.

I couldn't face killing all these wanna-be familiars. And it would be my job to do so. I'd get blamed for the theft(s), and I'd have to put down the creatures affected. It was the only way to negate the power of their poop.

She put her newly cleaned paw down on the concrete floor. "You couldn't 'put us down.'" She used great sarcasm on the phrase. "It would set the magical world back more than a hundred years. There wouldn't be enough of us to help your precious mages perform their silly little spells."

"Which might be the point of this attack," I said. "So tell me what you saw the last few days."

And why you never said a word, I almost added, but didn't.

"I'm not supposed to tell you anything. I'm not even supposed to talk with you."

Technically true. Familiars are only supposed to talk to their personal mages. But I get to hear and every one of them speak when they come into the store to make sure they really are familiars and not just plain old un-magical creatures looking for a free hand-out.

But Fiona had spoken to me before, mostly sarcastic comments about the store patrons. I'd tried pairing her up with a few, but she always had an under-the-breath comment that convinced me she and that mage wouldn't be a good match.

"I haven't seen anything," she said.

"What have you heard, then?" I asked.

"Nothing," she said. "The system is working just fine."

That sarcasm again, which lead me to believe she was leaving out a detail or two deliberately, hoping I would catch it.

Damn lions. They're just giant cats. They toy with everything.

And at that moment, Fiona was toying with me.

"But something's bothering you," I said.

"Not me so much." She picked up that clean right paw, turned it over, and examined the claws. "Roy."

Roy was the lion to her lioness. He wasn't head of the pride because there was no pride. We knew better than to get an entire pride of lions into that small habitat. No one would ever be able to see their individual natures—and no mage was tough enough to get that many catly familiars.

"What's bothering Roy?" I asked.

"Ask him."

"Fiona…"

She nibbled on one of the claws, then set her paw down again. "There was—oh, let me see if I can find the phrase in your language—an overpowering scent of ammonia."

"Ammonia?"

"And a very bright light."

"An explosion?" I asked. Fertilizer mixed with the right chemicals, including ammonia, created the same thing in both the magical and the non-magical world.

A bomb.

Only the magical bomb made of this kind of fertilizer didn't just destroy lives and property, it also cut through dimensions.

"It's not an explosion yet," she said. "He claims he has a sixth sense about things. Or did he say he can see the future? I forget exactly. But it was something like that."

"Or maybe he just knows something," I snapped.

"Or maybe he just knows something." She sounded bored. "He does say that because he's king of the jungle, the wanna-bes tell him things."

Which was the most annoying thing about Roy. He really believed that king of the jungle crap. Too much Kipling as a cub—or maybe too many viewings of the *Lion King.*

"I should really send you back to the habitat until this is resolved," I said to Fiona.

She hacked like she had a hairball, a sound she (sort of) learned from me. She thought it was the equivalent of my very Chicago, very dismissive "ach."

"I'd rather be out front, watching the floor show," she said.

And I sent her back out there because I had a soft spot for Fiona. Technically, I don't need a familiar. I have more than a thousand of them.

But if I did need one, I'd pick Fiona.

She knew it and she played on it all the damn time.

I waited until she was through that little curtain of light before I stepped through the hidden door into the habitat area.

It was always surprisingly quiet inside the habitat area. The first time I went in, I expected chirping birds and chittering monkeys and barking dogs—a cacophony of creature voices expressing displeasure or loneliness or sheer cussedness.

Instead, the area was so quiet that I could hear myself breathe.

It also had no smell—unless you counted that dry scent of air conditioning. The animal smells—from the pungent odor of penguins to the rancid scent of coyote—existed only in the individual habitat.

Just like the noises did.

If I went through the membrane on my left (and only I could go through those membranes—or someone I had approved, like the assistants), I would find myself in a cold dark cave that smelled of rodent and musty water. If I looked up, I'd see the twenty-seven bats currently in inventory.

We were always understocked on bats. Mages, particularly young ones raised in Goth culture, wanted bats first, wolves second, and cats a distant third. I'd given up trying to tell those kids to get some imagination.

I'd given up trying to tell the kids anything.

If I went through the membrane on my right, I'd slide on polar ice. Here the ice caps weren't melting. Here, my six polar bears happily fished and scampered and did all those things polar bears do—except that they didn't attack me. They didn't even bare their fangs at me.

I stopped between the two membranes and frowned. Whoever took the poop hadn't taken it from inside the habitats. It was simply too dangerous for the unapproved guest.

Hell, it was often dangerous for the assistants. I'd had more than one assistant mauled by a creature that didn't like the way he was looking at it.

And the poop was not registered as collected either. So whoever had taken it had spelled it out between gathering and delivery into the outside system.

I walked between dozens of habitats, trying to ignore the curious faces watching me.

I did feel for the wanna-bes. They were like children in an old-fashioned orphans' home. They hoped that someone would come to adopt them. They prayed that someone would come to adopt them. They were afraid that someone had come to adopt them.

And the only way they would know was if I brought them out of the habitat to the front of the store. (Except in the case of the dangerous exotics or the biting/stinging insects. In those cases, the mage had to enter the habitat without fear. *That* rarely happened either.)

Finally I got to the Serengeti Plain.

Or what passed for it in Roy and Fiona's habitat. It was kind of an amalgam of the best parts of a lion's world minus the worst part. Lots of water, lots of space to run, lots of space to hide. A great deal of sunshine and never, ever any rain.

I slipped through the membrane and, because of my past experience, paused.

The first step into Roy's world was overwhelming. The heat (about twenty degrees higher than I ever liked, even in the summer), the smell (giant cat mixed with dry grass and rotting meat from the latest kill), and the sunlight (so bright that my best sunglasses were no match for it—and as usual, I had forgotten any sunglasses) all made for a heady first step into this habitat.

More than one assistant had been so disoriented by the first step that Roy was able to tackle, stand on, and threaten the assistant in the first few seconds. After you've had several hundred pounds of lion standing on your chest, with his face inches from yours—so close you could see the pieces of raw meat still hanging from his fangs—you'd never want to go back into that habitat either.

Unless you're me, of course. I expected Roy to scare me that first time.

I didn't expect him to catch me off guard.

So when he did, I congratulated him, told him he was quite impressive, and warned him that if he hurt a human he'd never graduate from wanna-be to familiar.

And from that point on, he never jumped on me again.

But he always snuck up on me.

On this day, he wrapped his giant mouth around my calf. His teeth scraped against my skin, his hot breath moist and redolent of cat vomit. He'd been eating grass again. We were going to have change his diet.

"Hey, Roy," I said. "I hear you have a sixth sense."

He tightened his jaw just enough that the edges of those sharp teeth would leave dents in my flesh—not quite bites, not quite bruises—for days. Then he licked the injured area—probably an apology, or maybe just a taste for salt (I was instant sweat any time I came into this place).

Finally, he circled around me and climbed a nearby rock so that he would tower over me. If I weren't so used to his power games, he'd make me nervous.

"It's not a sixth sense," he said in an upperclass British accent. That accent had startled me when we were introduced. "So much as a finely honed sense of the possible."

"I see," I said, because I wasn't sure how to respond. I hadn't even been certain he would talk to me, and he'd done so almost immediately.

Which led me to believe the king of the jungle was more terrified than he wanted to admit.

"You realize I am only speaking to you," he said with an uncanny ability to read my mind (or maybe it was just that finely honed sense of what I might possibly be thinking), "because great evil is afoot, and I have no magical counterpart with which to fight it."

I almost said, *It's not your job to fight it,* but I didn't. I didn't want to insult the poor beast. Instead, I said, "That's precisely why I'm here. I figured you know what was going on."

"Bosh," he said. "Fiona told you. She has a thing for you, you know."

"A thing?" I asked.

"She wants to be your familiar." He opened his mouth in a cat-grin. "She doesn't understand—or perhaps she doesn't believe—that you have hundreds of us and as such do not need her."

I nodded because I wasn't sure what else to do. And because I was already thirsty. I'd forgotten not just my sunglasses but my bottle of water as well.

"Well," I said, "you do know what's happening, right?"

"Oh, bomb-making, dimension hopping, familiar murder—all the various possibilities." He laid down and crossed his front paws as if none of that bothered him. "And just you here because you seem to believe that you can save the world all by your own small self."

"With the help of your finely honed sense of the possible."

"That too." He tilted his massive head and looked at me through those slanted brown eyes.

My heart rate increased. Occasionally I still did feel like prey around him.

"Well?" I asked.

"Have you ever thought that your culprit isn't human?"

"No," I said. "Demons don't care about familiars. Only mages do."

"Really." He extended the word as if it were four. "Humans generally ignore scat, don't they?"

"Generally," I said. "We try not to think about it."

"And yet those of us in the animal kingdom find within it a wealth of information."

"Yes," I said. "But the amount of power it would take to complete this spell tends to rule out anything that isn't human."

He made the same hairball sound that Fiona did. They were closer than they liked to admit.

"You humans are such speciest creatures. It doesn't help that the mage gods allow you the choices and we have to wait until you make them. It leads me to believe that the mage gods are human—or were, at one point."

I wasn't there to discuss religion. "You're telling me, then, that your finely honed sense of the possible leads you to the conclusion that a familiar has done this."

"I didn't say that."

"A creature then. A magical creature of some kind."

He slitted his eyes, the feline equivalent of yes.

"But you have no evidence," I said.

"I have plenty of evidence. Consider the timeline. It took you forever to discover this theft, and yet no bomb has exploded. No one has made threats, and no mage has suddenly gained unwarranted power."

"That's not evidence. That's supposition."

He lifted his majestic head. "Is it?"

"So who do you suppose has stolen the poop—and why?"

He rested his head on his paws and continued to stare at me. "That's for you to work out."

"In other words, you don't know."

"That's correct. I don't really know."

"But you're not worried."

"Why should I worry? From my perspective, removing the scat is a prudent thing to do."

I hadn't expected him to say that. "What do you mean?"

He heaved a heavy, smelly sigh. "I'm a cat who lives in the wild. Think it through."

Then he jumped and I cringed as he headed right toward me. He landed beside me, chuckled and vanished through the tall grass.

He'd gotten me again. He loved that. He'd probably been planning to jump near me through the entire conversation, his back feet tucked beneath him and poised, even though his front half looked relaxed.

He wasn't going to give me any more. He felt he didn't need to.

Cats in the wild.

Cat poop in the wild.

Hell, cat poop in the house. Cats were all the same.

They buried their poop so no one could track them.

The problem wasn't the poop thief.

The poop thief was protecting the wanna-bes from something else. Something that tracked through scat.

Something that wasn't human.

I swore and bolted out of the habitat.

I needed my research computer, and I needed it now.

***

VERY FEW THINGS targeted familiars—or perhaps I should say very few non-human things. And I'd never heard of anything that targeted wanna-bes, because a wanna-be's power, while considerable, wasn't really honed.

Wanna-bes were, for lack of a better term, the virgins of the familiar world.

And nothing targeted virgins (not even those stupid civilian terrorists. They got virgins as a *reward*).

So when I got out of the habitat, I had the computer search for strange creatures or things that targeted virgins. I got nothing.

Except the search engine, asking me a pointed electronic question:

Do you mean things that prefer *virgins?*

And I, on a frustrated whim, typed *yes*.

What I got was unicorns. Unicorns preferred virgins. In fact, unicorns would only appear to virgins. In fact, unicorns drew their magic from virgins.

But the magic was pure and sweet and hearts and flowers and Hello Kitty and anything else treacly that you could think of.

Except if the unicorn had become rabid.

I clicked on the link, found several scholarly articles on rabies in unicorns. Rabid unicorns were slightly crazed. But more than that, they had no powers because no virgin (no matter how stupid) was going to go near a horse-sized creature that shouted obscenities and foamed at the mouth.

That was stage one of the rabies. Unlike rabies in non-magical creatures, rabies in unicorns (and centaurs and minotaurs and any other magical animal) manifested in temporary insanity, followed by darkness and pure evil.

The craziness, in other words, went away, leaving nastiness in its wake.

Minotaurs, centaurs, and other such creatures attacked each other. They stole from the nearest mage—or enthralled him, stealing his magic before they killed him.

But unicorns…

Unicorns still needed virgins.

And the only solution was to steal the powers of wanna-be familiars.

Provided, of course, that the unicorn could find them.

And unicorns, like most other animals, hunted by scat.

***

I WISH I COULD SAY I got my giant unicorn-killing musket out of mothballs and carried it through an enchanted forest, hunting a brilliant yet evil unicorn that wanted to devour the untamed magic of wanna-be familiars.

I wish I could say I was the one who shot that unicorn with a bullet of pure silver and then got photographed with one foot on its side and the other on the ground, leaning on my musket like hunters of old.

I wish I could say I was the one who cut off its horn, then snapped the thing in half, watching the dark magic dissipate as if it never was.

But I can't.

Technically, I'm not allowed to leave the store.

So I had to call in the Homeland Security—Magical Branch anyway. I could have called the local mage police, but I wasn't sure where this unicorn was operating, and HS-MB had contacts worldwide.

They found four rabid unicorns all in the same forest, somewhere in Russia, along with a few rabid squirrels (probably the source of the infection) and a rabid magical faun that was going around murdering all the bears for sport.

The unicorns died along with the squirrels and that faun. The poop reappeared in my computer system, and went back through the normal channels. That week, we made double our money on magical fertilizer, which was good since we'd made none the week before.

All seemed right with the magical world.

Except one thing.

I dragged Fiona to her habitat so I could confront both her and Roy.

They usually didn't spend much time together. They blamed it on not really having a pride, but I knew the problem was Fiona. She hated having to hunt for him, then watch him eat the best parts.

She hated most things about feline life and once muttered, as yet another well adjusted young mage took a domestic cat as her familiar, that she wished she were small and cute and cuddly.

She had to fetch Roy. He wasn't going to come. He hadn't even attacked me as I entered the habitat—probably because Fiona was with me.

I waited as he climbed to the top of his rock, then assumed the same position he'd been in before he jumped at me. Only this time I was prepared. I had my sunglasses and my water bottle.

I also stood a few feet to the right of my previous position, a place he couldn't get to from the top of that rock.

Fiona sat at the base of the rock, beneath the outcropping, in the only stretch of shade in this part of the plain.

"You want to tell me how you did it?" I asked when Roy finally got comfortable. He sent me an annoyed look when he realized that I had stationed myself outside of his range. "You knew that there was a rabid unicorn after wanna-bes, and you somehow got the entire group at Familiar Faces to cooperate with you, all without leaving your habitat."

Then I looked at Fiona. She had left the habitat. She left it every single day.

The tip of her tail twitched, and she tilted her head ever so slightly, her eyes twinkling. But she said nothing.

Roy preened. He licked a paw, then wiped his face. Finally he looked at me, the hairs of his mane in place, looking as majestic as a lion should.

"I am king of the jungle," he said.

This is a plain, I wanted to point out, but I didn't for fear of silencing him. Instead I said, "Yet some of the other familiars don't live in habitats like yours. The snakes, for example."

He yawned. "The unicorn wasn't after them."

"But the animals?" I asked.

He closed his great mouth, then leaned his head downward, so that his gaze met mine. "The Russian Blues are refugees. You didn't know that, did you?"

I got two domestic cats—purebred Russian Blues. Most purebred cats aren't familiars—they have the magic bred out of them with all the other mixed genes—but these Blues were amazing. And pretty. And not that willing to talk, even when they knew it was the price of gaining a mage.

"Refugees?" I said. "They were adopted before?"

"Their mages murdered by the new secret police for being terrorists. I thought you checked all of this out."

I tried to, but I never could. Animal histories weren't always that easy to find.

"They'd heard rumors about something rabid getting into an enchanted forest somewhere in deepest darkest Russia. Then some young familiars—what you call wanna-bes—withered and died as their powers were sucked from them over a period of months."

He tilted his head, as if I could finish his thought.

And I could.

"So the Blues suspected unicorns," I said.

"There were always rumors of unicorns in that forest," he said, "but of course, none of us had ever seen them. For normal unicorns, you need virginal humans. None of us had encountered abnormal unicorns before."

I did the math. The Blues had arrived last Thursday, which was the last day Carmen had worked before Tuesday, when she discovered the problem.

"You went into protect mode immediately," I said.

"It is my pride, whether you admit it or not."

I didn't admit it, but I understood how he thought so. He needed a tribe to rule, so he invented one.

"I still don't understand what happened. You don't have the magic to make other animals' poop disappear."

"But they do," he said.

"I know that." I tried not to sound annoyed. He was toying with me again. I hated being a victim of cat playfulness.

"So how did you tell them what to do?"

He opened his mouth slightly, in that cat-grin of his. Then he got up, shook his mane, and walked back down the rock. He vanished in the tall grass, disappearing against its browness as if he had never been.

"He could tell me," I said.

"No, he can't." Fiona hadn't moved.

I let out a small sigh. He hadn't been toying with me. She had.

"You did it," I said.

"Me and the bees," she said. "They're creating quite a little communications network with those hive minds of theirs. They send little scouts into the other habitats every single time you go from one to the other. The ants too. You really should be more careful."

I felt a little frisson of worry. I had had no idea. I didn't want the bees to get delusions of grandeur. I already had to deal with Roy.

"You told them to spread the word."

She nodded.

"And you told them how the animals could hide their poop."

She inclined her head as regally—more regally—than Roy ever could.

"Why?" I asked. "You had no guarantee of a threat."

"This is the biggest gathering of the Hopeful on the globe," she said. "Of course we are a target."

She was right. I sighed, took a sip from my water bottle, and frowned. This entire event had opened my eyes to a lot of scary possibilities, things I had never considered.

We were going to have to rethink the way we handled waste. We were going to have to protect the poop somehow, and I didn't want to consult HS-MB about that. They'd have to hold hearings, and the wrong someone could be sitting in.

I didn't want us to become a magical terrorism target, nor did I want us to be a target for every rabid unicorn in the world.

I would have to set up the systems myself.

"You need me," Fiona said, "whether you like it or not. You can't have pretend familiars. You need a real one."

She was making a pitch. Cats never did that. Or they only did so if they believed something was important.

"Why here?" I asked. "I've found you some pretty spectacular possible mage partners, and you've turned them down."

She wrapped her tail around her paws and stared at me. For a moment, I thought she wasn't going to answer.

Then she said, "This is my pride. Roy might think it his, but he's a typical lion. He thinks he's in charge, when I do all the work."

She raised her chin. That tuft of hair that all lionesses had beneath looked more like a mane in the shade than it ever had. It made her look regal.

"Well," she added, "I'm not a typical lioness, content to hunt for her man and to feel happy when he fathers a litter of kittens on her only to run them out when they threaten his little kingdom. I don't want children. And I want to eat first."

"You can do that with other mages," I said.

"But I won't have a pride. Don't you see? I'm the one who spoke to the Blues. I'm the one who keeps track of those silly mice—even though I want to eat them—and I'm the one who calms the elephant whenever she has the vapors. No one credits me for it, of course, but it's time they should."

No one, meaning me. I hadn't noticed, and Fiona was bitter. Or maybe she just felt that I wasn't holding up my end of the bargain.

"Besides," she said, "it's hot in here. Can we go back to the air conditioning?"

I laughed and stepped out of the habitat. She followed.

"I'll petition the mage gods," I said.

"I already did." She was walking beside me as we headed toward the front room. "They said yes. I put their response under the cash register."

We went through the portal. The mice were having a party on top of the cheese books. One of the snakes was dancing too, trying to come out of its basket like a charmed snake from the movies. The dance was a bit pathetic, since the snake was the wrong kind. It was the tiniest of my garden snakes.

They all stopped when they saw me. I looked toward the mall's interior. The customer door was closed and locked and the main lights were off. The closed sign sat in the window.

Carmen had gone home long ago.

I went to the cash register and felt underneath it. Some dust, some old gum—and yes, a response from the mage gods, dated months ago.

"You took a long time to tell me this," I said to Fiona.

She wrapped herself around the counter. "You should clean more."

Come to think of it, a few months before was when she really started muttering her protests out loud. In English. She was doing everything felinely possible except blurting it out that she was now my familiar.

I had never heard of a familiar picking a mage.

Although that wasn't really true. The familiars always made their preferences known. I knew how to read the signs. For everyone, it seemed, but me.

"Do you regret this?" Fiona asked quietly.

"Hell, no," I said. "Your brilliance averted a major international incident and saved the lives of hundreds of familiars."

"Don't you think that makes me deserving of some salmon?"

I almost said *I think that makes you deserving of anything you damn well please,* and then I remembered that I was talking to a cat. A large, independent-minded, magical cat, but a cat all the same.

"Salmon it is," I said and snapped a finger. A plate appeared with the thickest, juiciest salmon steak I could conjure.

I set it down next to her.

"Next time," she said, "you're taking me out."

"Restaurants don't allow animals," I said. "At least, not in Chicago."

"I wasn't talking about a restaurant," she said. "I meant a salmon fishery or perhaps one of those spawning grounds in the wild. I heard there's a species of lion who hunts those grounds."

"Sea lions," I said. "You're not related."

She chuckled, then wrapped her tail around my legs, nearly knocking me over. Affection from my lioness.

From my familiar.

However I had expected my day to end, it hadn't been like this.

Carmen was right. This day had been weird.

But good.

"So are you going to promise to take me to a fishery after the next time I save lives?" Fiona asked.

"I suppose," I said, wondering what I had gotten myself into.

Fiona licked her lips and closed her eyes. The mice started dancing all over again, and chimpanzees came out of the back to see what the commotion was.

After a weird day, a normal night.

And I found, to my surprise, that I preferred normal to weird.

Maybe I was getting soft.

Maybe I was getting older.

Or maybe I had just realized that I was a mage with a familiar, a powerful smart familiar, one I could appreciate.

One who would keep me and my animals safe.

One who would rule her pride with efficiency and not a little playfulness.

I could live with that.

I had a hunch she could too.

Domestic Magic

THE DREAM'S LIKE THE SCENES on TV only with magic. J. Rutherford Wisenhauer, the Third comes into the cafeteria wearing his father's black robes, points a finger at June Bauer and immediately she's burning. Alive. A couple other kids use water spells to put her out, but when they do, he shoots flames at them, and they go down.

Water spells are beyond the expertise of almost everyone in the room—one of the higher levels that a lot of us will learn in college (at least that's what Mrs. Parnham says. She also says don't worry about it; you won't ever need them, which is bad advice considering the dream).

I'm in line to pay for the slice of pizza I'm not supposed to be eating—Mom says you can't use magic to get rid of fat; it's not fair and it won't hold (which turned out to be true in the case of my older sister)—when J. Rutherford starts his rampage. I scurry behind the steam tables, taking my tray with me—God knows why I think pizza will be helpful—and I watch him burn down half a dozen other students before Principal

Haas, who is still in his office, douses the entire cafeteria in an ocean of water.

We—everyone in the cafeteria—get swept outside, but not before six die. They'll stay dead too. Resurrection spells are black magic, and worse than that, they're flawed. You create zombies or ghosts unless you're really, really good at it. So as drenched kids run across the lawn—slow motion, just like on TV—everyone knows that what happened in there was awful, permanent, and terrible.

And then I wake up.

In tears.

I'm not a precog. I don't have a lot of magic skills and the ones I do have are disgustingly domestic—I can turn McDonald's French fries into the best garlic mashed potatoes you've ever tasted; I can clean your house with an eye blink; I can iron your clothes just by rubbing my forefinger and thumb together. It's so damn sexist. Boys almost never get the domestic magic gene. Some of our geneticists (yes, we have geneticists and other scientists as well) think that the domestic magic gene is carried on the X chromosome and becomes stronger in girls than it'll ever be in boys.

So I've accepted that I have girl magic—the most stereotypical type. I've also accepted what I can't do.

Among the many things I can't do is see the future. Not in flashes, not in visions, and certainly not in dreams.

So no one is going to believe that what I dreamed might come true.

Maybe not even me.

But I'm scared too. Because if I did see the future, then I'm duty-bound to stop this thing.

Except I'm not the right person for the job. J. Rutherford and I have history.

Bad history.

The kind that makes anything I say about him sound suspiciously like I'm out for revenge.

Which I'm not.

At least, not any more.

***

J. Rutherford and I grew up on the same block. He lived three houses down from me in this single-story suburban ranch thing that everyone thinks is trendy now, but they thought it down market then.

His dad had just started the Magic Revival Hour on local cable access, but the show hadn't yet been picked up by the SyFy Channel, which led to repeat airings on USA, which made J. Rutherford Wisenhauer, the Second (known around here as Number Two) the most famous real magic proponent in the country.

That's when the Wisenhauers bought the mansion on Pendergast Hill, although you'd more properly call that white elephant a castle, and when the rumors about Number Two dabbling in the black arts started.

There's lots of jealousy in the magic community. My mom always attributed the comments to sour grapes—it was pretty clear from the beginning that Number Two's

TV show was going to take off, especially when the Conservative Right sent its minions from all over the country to picket outside his cable access studios.

But I wasn't so sure jealousy was the source of the talk. I'd seen J. Rutherford around the neighborhood and he knew how to do stuff long before it got taught in Salem Township Elementary. Mean stuff, too, like hanging someone by his feet from an invisible rope or morphing a litter of puppies into a single entity attached at the tips of the tails.

That stuff may not be black magic, but it is precursor black magic, and something most parents would never, ever allow their kids to read about, let alone try.

Some kids knew how to undo—which made me wonder about them too—and more than a few parents got involved, privately talking to Number Two or his wife. They always promised to do something—and they did, but only about the problem at hand. The puppies got separated or someone cut the invisible rope and floated the poor victim to the ground so he won't break anything.

But the Wisenhauers never really did anything about J. Rutherford and we all breathed a sigh of relief when he moved to that hilltop.

We figured he wouldn't be our problem any more.

But of course, he was.

***

As for me and J. Rutherford, here's the text message version. But first, you need a little background.

What most people don't know about small domestic magic is that it's practical magic. I can do all kinds of small useful things that no one else even thinks of. I can stop your casserole from burning, or add golf spikes to your shoes so you won't slip down an icy hill.

I'm like the white vinegar of magic; no one even thinks of me until they spill red wine on their shirt.

The thing I learned from my mother is that practical magic is subtle. I can't resuscitate a blackened banana into nutritious food, but I can prevent a perfect yellow banana from going stale for an entire week. And that's valuable, especially when you only have so much food, and it'll all spoil before you get to it.

Sometimes, by thinking small, you can make great changes.

Mom told me all this by way of a lecture one night after a long crying jag—mine, of course. I was upset because I couldn't make rats jump over the walls of their maze like show ponies. Everyone else could do it, but not me.

I, however, could clean their cages with a wave of a hand.

Mom said that cage cleaning is a lot more important to real life than rat wall-jumping, which of course I didn't believe. But she talked about the practical magic, subtle magic, small equals great thing, and I finally believed her.

Then I decided to test it on J. Rutherford.

Okay. I didn't decide right then and there, but the next day, I'm outside and I see J. Rutherford picking on the new kid from down the block.

The new kid looks pickable, the kind who just by his clothes is asking for trouble. He's wearing obvious hand-me-downs—the worn knees on his jeans actually puddle around his ankles—and he's way too skinny. He has a bruise along one chin and fragile glasses that someone has attached to his head with one of those rubber things that goes around the back of the skull.

To make things worse, he doesn't approach the world with confidence. He cringes as he walks, which is a neon red KICK ME sign to someone like J. Rutherford.

J. Rutherford has the new kid in his sights. He's calling to the kid, putting on the personal charm that he learned from Number Two, and making the kid feel welcome. I've seen J. Rutherford do this a dozen times, and it always ends badly.

Actually, it always ends with the invisible rope, and a kid hanging by his feet from some obscure spot in the neighborhood until someone sees him and gets him down.

Only I think this kid isn't going to survive the upside-down trick. It's going to break what little spine he has left.

I'm about to find a grown-up when I remember what Mom says about small things. I know magic theory. I know that the invisible items created—heck, any item created—has to be made of the same kind of materials it would have in the real world. Which is why, to go back to the banana example, I can't create a new banana from a spoiled one (my magic isn't big enough) but I can preserve a good one for a limited period of time.

J. Rutherford's invisible ropes are made of hemp. He's never been any good at tying those plastic ropes or those slick ropes you buy at the hardware store. He can only tie—and we're talking by hand here—the ropes made from coarse natural materials.

Now if I were better at magic, I'd change the natural ropes to plastic ropes, but I'm not. I have to think domestically.

I have to think small.

And as J. Rutherford conjures his invisible hemp rope, I stand on the curb, just outside his eye line and fray the weave. I fray it so badly the rope has no tensile strength at all. J. Rutherford doesn't notice because rough unfrayed hemp feels pretty much the same as rough frayed hemp, especially when you can't see what you're doing.

So he commands this thing, with its hangman's noose, to wrap itself around the new kid's feet. It does, but the minute J. Rutherford pulls the thing tight—that moment in which so many of us fell flat on our backs and screamed with surprise—the thing just kinda slips away from the kid's ankles, leaving rope burns and little else.

The kid still screams like the hounds of hell are after him, and runs home.

I slide along the curb until I find a good tree, and wait there, but J. Rutherford never sees me. Instead, he picks up the rope, and tries to figure out what went wrong.

He did that every single time I thwarted him—and I thwarted him a lot that spring. Then he finally gets the bright idea to make the rope visible (something the rest of us would have done right away; I never said J. Rutherford was the sharpest knife in the drawer) and sees the fraying.

Even then he doesn't figure out it's me. He blames a bunch of other kids. None of them know how to fray a magical rope like that—the magic is too small, and most people never learn the small stuff because it seems too unimportant.

So it takes him another month to find me.

But when he does....

Oh, when he does…

I don't like to remember that. It involved hanging—by the neck, actually—and real torture and six weeks in the hospital for me. By the time my throat had healed enough so that I could talk and my hands had healed enough so that I could write, Number Two had moved his family to their little castle and had given lots of money to local charities.

So when I blamed J. Rutherford, no adult believed me.

The kids did, of course. They knew how mean he could be.

But the adults wondered why I was lying about such a nice kid (he knew to turn on the charm with them too) and urged me to tell them what really happened.

The local police (magical branch) figured some drifter had done this. There'd been a lot of torture murders of little girls in nearby communities, and they figured this was just a different version of the same old song.

Only they caught the torture murderer guy, and he confessed to killing dozens of kids all over the country, but he wouldn't admit to attacking me.

Even after that, no adult believed me and the more I pointed at J. Rutherford, the more people forgot my six weeks in the hospital (and the very real fear that I wasn't going to survive) and the more they started thinking of J. Rutherford as the victim of some poor little girl's delusion.

Once I asked my mom if Number Two had cast a spell on the whole town, making them believe that J. Rutherford was a good kid.

But she just shook her head. "If he cast that kind of spell, you would never say anything about J. Rutherford, and I would think he's a saint too."

Still, I wondered if such a spell would work on people who'd suffered at J. Rutherford's hands. Maybe the spell only worked on people who hadn't paid much attention to J. Rutherford.

Only I didn't say that theory to Mom because she'd tell me to let it all go and to stay away from the Wisenhauers. It was just safer that way.

And I couldn't look up black magic spells without setting off alarms all over town. I was already seen as the kid who went crazy when that drifter tortured her. If I got viewed as the crazy kid who dabbled in black magic, I'd get sent away somewhere.

So I successfully avoided J. Rutherford for four years—from elementary school to our first year of high school—and I never talked about him.

But that didn't stop everybody else from wondering if I ever got over the "trauma." I have to see counselors every other week, and no matter how much I claim I'm over it, they don't believe me.

In fact, sometimes they act like I'm the one who's going to blow up the school—even though girls never do those things, not even at the magical schools.

Mom thinks I'm just paranoid—and she says that I'm not over it either and won't be until we move somewhere far away from the Wisenhauer family (although I wonder how that's possible to do, with Number Two being internationally famous and all).

So I'm just hanging on until I get out of high school. I'm hoping for college somewhere that'll appreciate my domestic talents or maybe even a trade school, like that magic chef school in Paris that I've been reading about.

At least, I was hanging on until the night I had that stupid dream.

***

THE FIRST TIME THE DREAM comes, it's at 3 a.m., and scares me so deep that I don't want to go back to sleep. So I go downstairs and make Mom the best breakfast ever—without magic (or much of it anyway). It's just the two of us now, with my older sisters married and making babies, and my dad long gone—as in he ran off, not as in he's dead.

I kinda like it being me and Mom, but I've never cooked anything just for her before, so when she gets up at her normal 5:30, she's stunned.

Over bacon, eggs, toast and this amazing pastry that I got from my latest French cookbook, I tell her about the dream and she says, "What an awful nightmare," which sounds like she's dismissing it.

So I say, "What if it's a premonition?"

And she stifles a laugh with a mouthful of scrambled eggs, probably thinking I don't notice.

"Honey, no one in our family has ever had precognitive abilities. Visions don't come to us. It's just not possible."

I set down my fork. The food is good, but not good enough to eat when I'm this upset. "What if you're wrong?"

She freezes for a minute, then sighs. "Has he said anything to you?"

"J. Rutherford? Are you *kidding*?"

"No," she says, but she's talking like she's not really paying attention to me. "So have the other kids said something, something you might have overheard?"

"You mean like J. Rutherford confessing his plans to his friends?" I can't keep my voice from rising. "Mom, that would mean he has friends."

She frowns at me. "You can't tell anyone about this, hon. Everyone knows that we don't have that kind of magic, and then there's your reputation."

She makes it sound like I did something wrong.

"I don't have a reputation," I snap.

"You know what I mean."

The thing is that I do know what she means. But that doesn't make it right. "*He* hurt *me*. How come everyone around here thinks I did something to him?"

"I didn't mean it that way, hon."

"But you said it that way."

"Just like the school officials will when you bring this to them." Mom leans over her plate of eggs. She hasn't touched the pastry yet and it's the best part. "Hon, listen. It makes sense that you'd have a nightmare about J. Rutherford. I'm amazed you don't have more of them."

"I do." I get up, grab my pastry and my coat and leave the house. Mom can handle the mess I made. And I don't need my books.

I just need to get out of there.

The one person who usually believes me, the one who understands me, and she tells me to blow this off. I'd love to, but I meant what I asked her.

What if this is a true premonition? What if I have developed some kind of Sight?

What if J. Rutherford walks into the cafeteria with a fire-loaded finger, and kills six of my classmates?

What if I could have prevented it just by telling the right person?

I don't want to live through that. I don't want to be the cause of six deaths.

I just don't.

***

So when I get to school, I go straight to the counselor's office. I have a private therapist, Mr. Marx, on Tuesdays outside of school, but my every-two-weeks meetings are with Mrs. Emerson who works in the guidance office. She doesn't have a psychology degree. Her degree is in magical brain phenomenon, which is more like neurology and psychiatry as it pertains to magic.

Or that's how she explained it to me once.

Mrs. Emerson is younger than my mom and skinnier too. She wears designer rip-offs, which automatically makes her suspect to me because I think anyone who wears designer rip-offs has to have low self-esteem.

But still, she's the only person with some authority I can think of telling. Or, to clarify, the only person with some authority who has even the slightest chance of believing me.

Her office has windows that overlook the parking lot. She has covered those windows in plants, many of which are hanging medicinal herbs. She makes me sit in that fake leather chair across from her desk and she listens attentively as I tell her about the dream and my fears. I don't tell her what Mom said, although Mrs. Emerson repeats Mom's sentiments almost word-for-word.

(Except she doesn't say our family; she says your family. But still.)

So I lie. I tell Mrs. Emerson she's one of the people burned to death.

That at least makes her stop offering petty reassurances. For a half a second she even looks a little scared.

Then she says, "You know, with all the recent television coverage of school shootings, it's not surprising you'd dream about something like that here. And as focused as you are on J. Rutherford Wisenhauer, it makes sense that he'd be the villain in your dream."

I stand up. I'm so mad that I can hardly see. I knew no one would take me seriously, and here they are, not taking me seriously.

"It's not a dream," I say. "At best, it's a nightmare. At worst, it's true."

That scared look comes back on her face and stays there longer this time. Then she gets up and goes to the filing cabinets behind her desk. She pulls open one in the middle, waves a hand over it so that I can't even see the folders, and peers inside.

She heaves a small sigh of relief, closes the drawer, and comes back to her desk.

"He doesn't have the ability to create fire like that," she says. "None of the students do."

"What about the teachers?" I ask.

She shakes her head. "That's a black magic."

"No, it's not," I say. "It's been around longer than almost all magic. The ability to make a flame so that you can light a room or ignite kindling to keep the family warm. It's a survival skill."

Which makes it a domestic magic. A small magic. I hope she doesn't figure that out. Because then that would turn the suspicion back on me.

Her jaw hardens and she says, "Is there anything else you'd like to tell me?"

Meaning am I planning this thing? As if my ability to create a tiny flame could turn into those jets of fire that I saw in my dream.

I decide to misunderstand her, even though I want to scream at her. There's a lot I want to tell her, much of which might get me expelled.

I walk to the door, put my hand on the knob, and then stop. "I just want to tell you this. If he does spray up the school and kill a bunch of people, it's not my fault. I've tried to warn you. If you die at lunchtime, it'll be your own damn fault."

Then I let myself out, only to find myself grabbed by two of the school's four security guards.

They pull me into the principal's office. Seems half of what I said in Mrs. Emerson's office sounded like a threat, so she pressed some button, notifying them. Now they're detaining me.

The good part is I'm not going to the cafeteria today.

The bad part is that I've only managed to make my crazy victim reputation worse.

Which means no one will believe me now.

And the longer this day goes on, the more I think they should.

***

OF COURSE NO ONE TALKS to J. Rutherford to see what he's planning. So when they finally let me out of Principal Haas's office with a warning not to threaten counselors again and a reminder that they'll be watching all of my interactions with authority figures, I realize that only one person can prevent this whole thing.

Me.

By the time they let me out of Principal Prison, it's long past lunch. No one's in the caf and no one will be again until tomorrow morning at 10:40 when the first lunch begins.

And nothing happened, which means everyone'll say that my dream was a nightmare and nothing more.

But there wasn't a timeline on the dream. It could've happened today or it might happen tomorrow.

Or, if I'm being charitable, it might never happen.

And that would be the best.

But it is a function of what I think about J. Rutherford that makes me believe he will attack the school and he'll do it sooner rather than later.

So as soon as they let me out of Principal Prison, I scout the hallways. I'm looking for J. Rutherford, and I find him in the library, actually cracking a book.

He's a lot bigger than he was when he put me in the hospital. He's six-five and built like a football player, even though he's not that athletic. He dresses in black, but that doesn't mean much since half the school does.

What he doesn't have are tats or piercings or other things that would scare the grownups. All he has are those sharp blue eyes that, if anything, have gotten meaner.

I stop at the door. My heart is pounding. I haven't voluntarily gotten near J. Rutherford in four years. But I'm going to do it now.

I square my shoulders and walk across the thick pile carpet until I reach his table. He's looking at old spell books—studying them in fact—and I can't tell if it's for a class or because he wants to.

He doesn't look up when I sit down. So I lean forward and put my hand over the page he's studying. Dust rises from the parchment.

He raises his head slowly and when his gaze meets mine, I nearly run from my seat.

It takes all of my strength to stay there.

"I know what you're planning," I say. "Don't do it."

He frowns.

"It'll hurt you more than anyone else." Which isn't technically true—the kids that burn alive and survive will always remember it even though healing magic'll ensure that their skin won't scar and the kids that die, well, their families'll be hurt the worst.

But my lie sounds good.

For a moment, tears line his eyes, then they disappear as quickly as they appeared.

"What are you talking about?" he snaps.

"Is this spellbook about the black arts?" I ask. "Is that how you learn the fire jet spell?"

His cheeks flush. For a moment—just a moment—he looks as terrified as Mrs. Emerson did.

Then he slams the book closed, right on top of my hand, and says in a really loud voice, "How come you always accuse me of stuff? I haven't done anything to you. I've *never* done anything to you."

Everyone turns and stares at us. I can see them out of the corner of my eye. But I don't look away from J. Rutherford, and I say softly, "We both know that's not true."

He starts to say something, but that's when my personal security guards—the same creeps that took me to Principal Prison—grab my arms again and drag me back there.

I get a lecture on harassing other students, and when I'm not repentant (I'm angry; no one is believing me), that's when I get suspended.

For three days.

Like I'm the bad guy.

Which I most decidedly am not.

***

THREE DAYS AWAY FROM SCHOOL—Wednesday, Thursday, Friday—and then the weekend. I figure nothing's going to happen this week, because I'm not there, and I'm absolutely there in the dream, right down to rescuing my own personal slice of pizza because I somehow deem it important.

Mom is "disappointed" in me and she actually makes me go see Mr. Marx like I'm the one who's crazy, not J. Rutherford.

Mr. Marx is, at least, sympathetic. But I have a hunch that's because the insurance company pays him more than $100 an hour to be as nice to me as he can.

Still, he says all the right things and makes me choke up when he says, "That took a lot of courage to face J. Rutherford by yourself."

He's right. It did take a lot of courage. More courage than I thought I had. But I really believe lives are at stake.

He also says, "You've done everything you can. You've warned the principal and the administration, you've even challenged J. Rutherford himself. There's not much more you can do."

And he's right about that too. Because I can't spell away J. Rutherford's powers nor can I dunk him in water every five seconds. I can't get those stupid school security guards to follow him and I don't have enough magic to fight him.

I've warned everyone and no one's listening.

"So now what am I supposed to do?" I ask Mr. Marx.

He shrugs. "It's a tough situation. Let's just hope everything you've done changes the tide."

It sounds like he believes me. In fact, when he said that I *thought* he believed me. But as I'm leaving I realize he never actually said that. In fact, he was careful not to say he believed me.

I've got to say Mr. Marx is pretty good at making me feel like I've had a sympathetic ear. But a sympathetic ear isn't what I want. I want someone to stop J. Rutherford. Or I want someone to prove to me that J. Rutherford isn't about to finger-burn kids in my school.

I'm depressed again by the time I get home. Depressed and angry and frightened.

So I do what any good old domestic magician does when she loses control of her world.

I cook and cook and cook. I use real recipes and I cheat on a few others. I make pastries and cakes and pies and two different dinners and a salad that has both fruit and vegetables and a dressing I invent myself.

I cook until I can't any more. (And Mom eats until she can't any more.)

Then I stagger to bed, so exhausted I know that nothing will ever wake me up.

***

EXCEPT THAT STUPID DREAM.

I have it again. Only this time, when J. Rutherford comes into the cafeteria, he looks right at me and his eyes are filled with tears.

But he doesn't point at me or at Jane Bauer. He starts with a different kid, a boy I don't recognize, and then when the same kids try to help, J. Rutherford goes after them.

I still manage to hide behind the steam tables, only this time I don't rescue my piece of pizza. And it takes the same amount of time for Principal Haas to get his act together and drown the entire cafeteria in water.

I wake up even more terrified, and this time, I wake up Mom. She's starting to worry now too, and she promises, in the morning, we'll hire a true precog and see exactly what is going on.

***

THE TRUE PRECOG is Willard Pruitt, the great-great-grandfather of last year's prom queen, Willa Pruitt. No one knows how old Willard is, but everyone knows he's the best precog in a family full of them.

He shows up at our house fifteen minutes early (Mom later jokes that precogs never do anything on time), banging on the door before I finish making Mom's breakfast. So I have to use a bit of magic to double everything, just so I can offer him some.

When he comes into the kitchen, I'm glad I made the effort. He's has that weird look some old guys get when it's pretty clear they were really big once and aren't any more. It's not that his clothes don't fit—they do—it's just that they look like the kind of clothes a six-six guy would wear instead of a guy who's a little under five-seven.

His bones are big too—his hands are twice the size of mine, but look frailer some how—and so is his nose. Hairs grow out of it and out of his ears, and when he sits at the table, he says, "I've been looking forward to this meal all week."

Which, I was about to say, was impossible, until I realize that he probably knows everything that's going to happen at this meeting. That creeps me out and makes me not want to talk to him.

Instead, I give him a serving of waffles sprinkled with powdered sugar and covered with strawberries so fresh they look like they've been airbrushed. He asks for and gets coffee, then he loads the waffles with butter and eats like he hasn't seen food in a week.

Mom and I wait until he's finished before telling him why we've called.

He listens, but with that distracted air people get when you're telling them something they already know.

Finally, I say, "You know how this is going to come out. Why don't you just tell us?"

He smiles, grabs the full orange juice glass in front of his empty plate, and leans back in his chair.

"Precognition isn't quite like that," he says. "Some events are certain—like this spectacular breakfast—and others are in flux. I have no idea what is going to happen in your school cafeteria, if anything. I am not privy to the future of the Wisenhauer family. It's blocked. It's always been blocked, which leads me to believe Number Two cast some kind of shield spell over the whole family about the time he decided to do his cable-access show."

For some reason that news makes me shudder.

"So," Willard Pruitt says, "I'm here partly to see if I can help you, partly to see if there's any truth to your dream, and partly for that breakfast. You should open a restaurant, honey. You're the best chef I've ever encountered."

I flush in spite of myself.

Mom nods.

"Yes," she says. "My daughter is an amazingly talented domestic."

I look at her in shock, thinking maybe she's talking about one of my sisters. Only my sisters aren't domestics. So Mom has to be talking about me. Except she's never talked about me like that before.

"What she isn't," Mom is saying, "is a visionary or a precog. This dream of hers, while scary, can't be true. Our family doesn't have the magic for it."

Willard Pruitt clears his throat. Then he drinks some orange juice. Then he clears his throat again.

He's obviously thinking about something, and he's battling with himself about whether or not to say it.

Finally, he says, "There're precogs and people who have a bit of the visionary magic, and then there's everyone else."

Mom nods. She knows this. *I* know this.

"But then there are break-through moments. Do you know what those are?"

Mom frowns. I frown. I've never heard of this.

"Break-through moments are future moments so powerful that even the non-magical get a sense of them. That's why the non-magical talk about having déjà vu. They've had a wisp of a vision about that moment, and haven't even acknowledged it on a conscious level. Usually they can't acknowledge it—they don't have the tools to access it."

I'm beginning to feel like I'm in magical theory class. All this talk about stuff most of us just do irritates me and gives me a headache all at the same time.

But I'm trying to pay attention to Willard Pruitt because he is, after all, trying to help me.

"The magical," he's saying, "no matter what their talents, can have these break-through moments and can remember them. Usually they come in a vision, not a dream and usually—forgive me hon…"

And he looks at me for that.

"…usually, they're about the visionary's impending death."

I let out a small breath. That revelation doesn't really surprise me. I had a hunch this might be about my death. Although that doesn't explain why I can see how the whole thing resolves—from the ocean of water the principal unleashes to the drenched kids running across the schoolyard in slow motion.

Mom picks up her coffee mug, spills some coffee, and sets it down again.

Willard Pruitt looks at her shaking hands, then reaches over and pats them. "I do not think your daughter is having a break-through moment."

Mom purses her lips and I can tell she's thinking he's patronizing her.

"This could be a sending, a warning, that's coming directly to her, something that could happen. Or it could be, as her counselor says, a manifestation of your daughter's fear of this young man which is—"

And he looks at me again.

"—entirely justified. The Wisenhauers are terrifying people, and they get away with a lot."

I let out a small sigh. He's the only person, except maybe Mom, who has ever really believed me.

"I happen to think, however, that it's a metaphor."

I blink. We're not in English class. Metaphor is not a word I expected this nice old guy to say.

"A metaphor?" Mom asks.

"Your daughter sees a potential in young Mr. Wisenhauer. She understands how destructive he is. Her subconscious is sending messages to her conscious via dreams, using the imagery of modern life. This doesn't mean that young Mr. Wisenhauer is going to destroy her school, but he is going to damage something important. Something important to your daughter. It's not by accident that she has this dream about the cafeteria, which is the only place in a high school where her talents are relevant. He's messing inside her magic, and the fact that in the first dream, she saves her food is important. How important I do not know. I think you should hire a dream interpreter. Then you'll get to the bottom of this."

A dream interpreter. I can see dollar signs in the sadness on Mom's face. Willard Pruitt is already costing us a small fortune. We can't afford any other help.

"What's a sending?" I ask. He had mentioned that first, before all the other possibilities.

He sighs, as if he had hoped I hadn't heard that part.

"A sending," he says, "comes from someone else. Like a message or a warning. It too can be a metaphor."

"How do I know if it's my subconscious or someone trying to contact me?" I ask.

"Well, you can hire someone to trace the dream to its source. It's a highly specialized form of magic. No one here has that ability, but I can give you some names—"

"What about you? Why can't you do it?" Mom asks.

"If it's not a vision or a true prophecy or a breakthrough moment, my magic can't help you either."

Her cheeks are flushed. Mom is getting mad. Next thing you know, she's going to deny him his fee, which she can't do since he already told us some valuable things.

And, I think, he's probably the only person who really, truly believes me. That's worth the fee too.

"Can I do anything to see if it's a sending?" I ask. "I mean, there's got to be a way to tell if it's just a dream or a sending, right, without going to the source?"

He looks at me for a long time. Then he says, "You might try dedicated dreaming."

He doesn't have to explain that to me. We all learn dedicated dreaming in Head Start. Naptime is supposed to be about dedicated dreaming, although you learn later in the biology of magic that four-year-olds really can't control their dreams. That ability doesn't come until puberty. But it's a good way to get little kids to close their eyes for a half an hour.

Dedicated dreaming, not that I've tried it since I became of age, is the ability to control your dreams. If it's a true dream, you can turn it, make it into what you want. You can even ask the dream questions and it'll answer you.

Essentially, dedicated dreaming is about talking to your own subconscious and having it answer.

So I can see the logic of his suggestion. If I can control the dream, then my subconscious is trying to tell me something. If I can't, then there's a good chance something else is going on.

Mom sighs. "Now I'm finally beginning to understand how all the mundanes feel."

By mundanes, she means the non-magical. I don't ask her what she means—I know Mom, and I know she makes comments like this as a setup for some angry comment.

But Willard Pruitt doesn't know Mom at all, so he asks her what she means.

She glares at him. "This all sounds like mumbo-jumbo. It's a colossal waste of time and—"

"Mom," I say.

He's leaning back, startled at the vehemence in her tone.

"—a waste of money and if we hadn't already paid you—"

"Mom!"

"—we wouldn't be."

"Which is why," he says as he stands up, "I always ask for up-front payment. It doesn't take a precog to know that sometimes customers don't want to hear what you have to say."

He nods at me, and I see warmth in his eyes.

"Good luck," he says softly. "The future is dark on this topic. I hope your dream is wrong, but if it's right, I know you will do the best you possibly can."

Note he doesn't say I would do the right thing. Or even that I would do the heroic thing. Only that I would do my best.

Which I'm already trying to do.

Mom's still yelling at him as he heads for the door. I stay and clean the kitchen, feeling unsettled by the encounter. Not because Mom is angry—she always gets angry when she feels like we spent money we don't have—but because, really, Willard Pruitt has no idea if my dreams predict the future or not.

He only has what we have—an idea that they don't, and a fear that they might.

I'd be back to square one if it weren't for two things: he actually believes (like I do) that J. Rutherford is a threat; and I can try dedicated dreaming.

When I finish cleaning my mess, I go upstairs and log onto our household computer. I read all I can find on dedicated dreaming, and there's not a lot, at least from the magical perspective.

What there is is all about ritual, the kinda stuff I usually scoff at.

But I need to know, so I go through all the goofy rituals from the scented oil bath to the vanilla candles to the overturned mirrors and the quiet bedroom. I'm prepared to have the dreams of my life.

And of course, I don't dream at all.

***

UNTIL SUNDAY NIGHT, the night before my suspension ends. I was right about one thing; nothing happened while I was away. School lunch is normal, and nothing, not even threats, make the news. I monitor the MySpace pages of everyone I can think of, and don't even see rumors.

Which both relieves me and terrifies me. It leads me to believe I'm onto something when in fact, I might just be delusional.

Certainly the fact that I can't even dedicated dream makes me wonder if I have much magic at all. According to the websites, dedicated dreaming is one of those basic spells everyone can perform after a certain age.

Everyone but me, apparently.

So I don't go through the stupid dedicated dreaming rituals at all on Sunday and I actually fall asleep on the couch, watching some Monster Truck Rally thing.

One minute I'm watching giant trucks drive over other giant trucks, and the next I'm back in the cafeteria, holding onto my silver tray with its lonely little piece of pizza. Kids are sitting at various tables, talking, and Mrs. McGuillicuty—the cafeteria supervisor—is telling me about this luscious lemon pie she makes, and I'm pretty convinced none of that happened before, but I'm not sure I'm making the changes.

So I consciously chose to set down my tray (and its delectable piece of pizza) and I turn around long before J. Rutherford comes into the cafeteria.

In fact, I'm beginning to think he's not going to when he does, his father's black robes flapping around him. J. Rutherford raises that deadly finger and then he stops. He stares at me.

I stare at him and realize how stupid he looks, all in black like a TV magician, with one finger pointed and this frown of concentration on his face. He's conjuring up how to do the spell, that's what he's doing.

And no one can stop him.

Except…

I wave a finger at Mrs. McGuillicuty's asbestos gloves, the ones she keeps behind the counter for removing things like pizza from the double-hot ovens. I command those gloves to cover J. Rutherford's hands and not to come off until he leaves the cafeteria, and gives up his dream of killing people.

The gloves soar across the caf just as he turns toward Jane Bauer, the kid he burned alive in the first dream. And as the fire jets out of his finger, the gloves slide on, interrupting the flow. Jane's clothes light on fire, the boys around her put it out, and those evil security guards— the ones that took me to Principal Prison—cart J. Rutherford away.

Then I wake up.

The TV's playing some Japanese game show, the point of which seems to be to make everyone fall so that their back bends into an unnatural position. Mom's covered me with a blanket, but she hasn't sent me to bed.

And my heart is pounding.

Okay. That had to be dedicated dreaming since I set down my tray and actually stopped J. Rutherford with domestic magic. That couldn't happen in real life.

I push off the blanket and go into the kitchen, my domain. There I drink some water, wipe off my sweaty face, and lean against the counter for a while.

It's done. The whole dream thing is over.

At least, I hope it is.

Especially as I head for school that morning.

And walk into the cafeteria at lunch.

***

OF COURSE, STUPID ME, I decide to have pizza to celebrate. I've been dreaming of pizza for a week now, and I deserve some. I mention that to Mrs. McGuillicuty as I'm getting my slice. She pulls off her asbestos gloves to serve it to me, fresh and bubbly, looking better than I even dreamed it would.

Then she tells me about this lemon pie she's making, and the hair rises on the back of my neck.

I turn just as J. Rutherford comes into the caf. Only he's not wearing his dad's robes and he's being trailed by those evil security guards. They're not quite touching the backs of his arms.

He comes directly at me. I snap my fingers, and instantly, I'm holding those asbestos gloves instead of my cafeteria tray.

He sees that move and he smiles. Then he blinks hard. Against tears.

Tears again from J. Rutherford Wisenhauer the Third. What the heck is this all about?

He crowds so close to me that I wedge my back against the railing around the steam tables.

"I just had to tell you," he says, "I've turned myself in."

He says it real soft, so no one else can hear, except maybe those guards.

My mouth is dry.

"The gloves got me," he says. "Good move. Made me realize that not all magic is about power. And some day, we're going to tell that to my dad."

Before I can even say, "Huh?" he heads out of the cafeteria again. Next thing I know it's all over the school that J. Rutherford Wisenhauer the Third has voluntarily committed himself to some treatment facility for suicidal kids. Suicidal magical kids.

Seems he'd been dreaming about dying for a week or more because (rumor has it) he can't stand living with Number Two and Number Two's expectations.

Only I know different. Maybe he's been dreaming of suicide, but only after he takes out part of the school.

Because he was sending me the dreams.

Me, the person he beat up so bad I went to the hospital.

Me, the person with such small magic that no one pays attention to it.

Me, the person who used that small magic to stop him once before.

The whole thing is a big scandal—the kind the tabloids love: J. Rutherford The Second's namesake is so miserable he's thinking of suicide. What's really happening in that mansion on the hill? Rumors of black magic, Satanism—and all that stuff the mundanes are afraid of.

When really, Mom thinks it was just the same stuff that mundanes deal with. A depressed kid, a distant and demanding father, an alcoholic mother (yep, that came out too). The kid decides he's going to go out, but in a way that'll destroy his father forever.

It's not enough to kill Number Two, after all. J. Rutherford has to demolish everything Number Two stands for.

Only some spark in J. Rutherford's subconscious, some little teeny part of himself, maybe the part that started all that self-loathing in the first place, knows it's wrong. So it sends out feelers to the one person who actually knows J. Rutherford for who he really is.

Lucky me.

J. Rutherford'll be in his mental health facility for the next five years or so. His father's not on TV any more, and the mansion's up for sale.

I've been accepted to the magical version of Le Cordon Bleu in Paris, and Mom, she vacillates between being really proud of me and wondering what she'll do when she no longer has a resident chief cook and bottle washer.

And I try not to do much dreaming. Sleep dreaming, that is. I'm up a little later than I used to be and I drink a lot more caffeine.

Mr. Marx says it's a natural reaction to all I've been through. Mom thinks I should get past it because dreaming's a normal part of life.

But I just don't want the responsibility. Or the angst over the life-and-death philosophical questions.

I'd rather just spend my life cooking—and not mopping up someone else's spilled red wine.

Say Hello
To My Little Friend

H E WAS STRANGE from the start, yet oddly compelling. I can explain the strange. The compelling is harder.

He'd come into my bar about 3:30 Friday afternoons, thirty minutes before the official start of Happy Hour. He'd take a seat as far from the door as he could get. He'd order two drinks—one, a piña colada, the other, light beer on tap.

Then he'd wait.

He was stunningly handsome. That's the thing you'd see first off. The square jaw, the black-black hair, the laughing blue eyes all accented his broad shoulders and perfect male model physique. Only he dressed like a regular guy: nice suit with a jacket he'd remove when he sat down, white shirt, and shoes that could use some attention. Before the drinks arrived, he'd loosen his tie and roll up his sleeves, revealing muscular arms.

And then he'd nurse the beer.

Any red-blooded woman would look at him, as well as a handful of closeted males. So of course I looked at him. I'm as red-blooded as the next woman—even if it is my bar.

I'm red-blooded, but not pretty. I'm perfectly cast in my role as bar owner. I'm muscular and broad-shouldered too. My father used to say I looked like Bette Davis—and he didn't mean the young beauty of her early roles. He meant the battle-axe from "Whatever Happened to Baby Jane?" with the crumpled skin and the bugged out eyes and the voice that sounded like she'd smoked a thousand cigarettes too many.

A few men like this look. They figure I'm easy (I'm not) because I'm lonely (I'm not that either), and they try to woo me with lies. The occasional guy who enjoys my friendship takes it a stage farther, but we usually agree to go back to platonic after a few months.

Men who look like this guy never give me a second glance. And if one of them had slept with me by accident (and none of them had), it would have been an invitation that came at last call, and the night would end with him chewing his arm off in the morning.

I know that. So when I started talking to Mr. Weird But Beautiful, I did it not because I wanted him (even though I did). I did it because he looked like he needed some advice.

To understand why he needed some advice, you need to know what my bar looks like. It's not a fern bar or a sports bar. There are no big screens scattered around, all turned to

ESPN. There are no giant booths with huge backs because I don't want couples making out in my place and getting us slapped with violating the decency laws.

There are round tables of various sizes scattered across the floor, and they get pushed aside on Saturdays, when my favorite DJ comes in to spin the tunes—usually oldies, because I don't tolerate that hip-hop crap in my bar.

The rest of the time, it's the juke that's been here since I bought the place. A pool table against the back wall gives the regulars a reason to return besides my lovely presence.

The bar's the first thing you see when you come in the door. The back bar is large and mirrored, so it looks like we have even more booze than we do. I put the expensive stuff back there because the business travelers who've just had a meeting in the big conglomerate across the street make it worth my while.

The bar is a classic U and made of expensive wood with a polyurethane top, so that I can wipe the thing off every night. Everyone vies for the twenty bar stools that surround the outside of the U, and during Friday Happy Hour, the line for those stools can be five deep.

Although it's not fair to call them stools. They're actually tall chairs with rounded backs that hug the backside of whoever's sitting there. I bought the things from a bar going out of business about five years ago, and they're the best purchase I ever made. They keep the hard drinkers—the guys who pass out with predictable regularity—in their chairs. These guys don't fall four feet to the floor, hitting their head on the bar rails on the way down and thinking lawsuit when they finally wake up.

Guys who drink like that—and every neighborhood bar has them—keep our local taxi service in business, especially weekend nights. I don't even have to call any more. At closing, half a dozen cabs show up here like they've been summoned. I confiscate keys, pour the hard drinkers into the cabs, and sign the tab. Then when the drinkers come back for their cars, I won't hand over the keys until I get reimbursed.

It works for all of us, and rarely does the hard drinker get mad.

I take care of my people. That's what I'm known for.

Which is why no one was surprised when I started talking to Mr. Weird But Beautiful.

He started coming in long about February, with that uncomfortable look most first timers in a bar often have. He wore a shiny silk suit and a matching silver tie, and he looked good enough to eat.

When he sat at the bar, I was surprised. When he ordered his light beer and piña colada, I waited for the pretty business associate to show up for their meeting.

Only she never came. The beer got nursed and the piña colada disappeared, although I never saw him take a sip.

And as the bar filled up, a bottle blonde stopped beside the empty chair, leaned against the bar, and displayed her assets prettily for him. After she ordered, she turned to him, and he smiled one of those Tom Cruise mighty megawatt smiles, the kind that makes you hot just thinking about it.

She smiled back and I could tell she was feeling like I was feeling—the right word and she was his.

He had one of those deep Barry White voices which carried even though he probably didn't intend it to.

Her eyes danced and she leaned in, just a bit, as he said, "Please say hello to my little friend."

Then he looked down.

She flushed, grabbed her drink, and left the bar.

And he leaned back, looking very confused.

Now most guys, when they have a pick-up line that fails, try another one. And any guy who looks like him doesn't need a line at all.

It was a testament to his attractiveness that no woman ever dumped a drink on his lap or slapped him or called him names. Every woman he approached—and by April, he was approaching the desperate ones as well as the pretty ones—gave him that what-the-hell-did-you-just-say? look and fled.

But he never varied his line, he never altered his routine, and he never ever got anyone to say hello to his little friend.

Until, of course, me.

***

IT WAS JUST AFTER EASTER when I finally had enough. When you have regulars in your place, you develop an emotional attachment to them. Sometimes that attachment is loathing, sometimes it's friendship, and sometimes it's pity.

With Mr. Weird But Beautiful, I found myself feeling oddly responsible. I wanted to sit next to him and say, "What? Your mother never taught you manners?"

But I knew that wasn't the way to approach him.

Instead, I pulled a bar stool over to his other side, the side away from the empty stool he hogged every Friday, and said, "Your little friend routine doesn't work."

He looked at me like he didn't know I could speak English. Maybe he thought the only sentences in my repertoire were "Light on tap and piña colada, right?" and "That'll be six-sixty-five."

It seemed to take him a minute to process this new sentence, and then he said, "It's gotta work."

"Nonsense," I said. "You need a new line, that's all. Half the women in this place would go home with you if you asked them right."

"I don't want them to go home with me. I want them to go home with Marty."

That's when I sighed. I couldn't help it. "Look," I said, "to get them home with Marty, you need to charm them first."

"No," he said. "That's not fair. *Marty* needs to charm them."

"Marty can work his magic in the privacy of your own bedroom," I said. "You—."

But by that time, Mr. Weird But Beautiful was giving me the what-the-hell-did-you-just-say? look. He flushed and he was starting to get out of his chair when I grabbed his wrist.

His muscular oh-so-strong wrist.

"I'm trying to help you here," I said. "It's been nearly three months, and you can't get a girl to spend thirty seconds with you. You're going about it wrong."

He pulled his wrist from my grasp. "First, I don't want her to spend time with me. I'm trying to fix up Marty. Second, Marty and I do not share a bed or even a house. Third, what the hell even makes this your business?"

"Nothing, I guess," I started, but by the time I finished the third word, he was gone.

Without paying for his beer or his piña. And, as usual, the beer was barely touched, but the piña was gone.

It really bugged me that I never saw him drink it.

Especially this time. When I was sitting beside him from the moment I set the drinks down.

***

I FIGURED THAT WAS THE LAST I'd see of Mr. Weird But Beautiful, so I wrote off the drinks and went back to my routine. No one asked after him, even though a few of the regulars noticed he was missing.

These were the closeted guys, one of whom got very drunk on a Friday in March, sidled up to Mr. Weird But Beautiful, and said, "I'll say hello to your little friend" in a suggestive voice, and nearly got tossed across the room.

Mr. Weird But Beautiful left after that too, although that time he paid, hands shaking. He did come back, though, the following week, and when his closeted stalker came up to him a second time, Mr. Weird But Beautiful held up his hand.

"Look," he said in a polite voice, the same voice he used for his pick-up line. "I vote Democrat. I believe in equal rights. I know we should be flattered because you're probably a very nice man. But believe me when I say that my friend and I are not your type."

The closeted stalker nodded once, then went back to his chair, probably trying to maintain some dignity. He never approached Mr. Weird But Beautiful again, but he did watch from time to time, maybe hoping Mr. WBB might change his mind.

Although I could have told him that he wouldn't. A guy who doesn't change his pick-up line is not going to change his orientation, no matter how much the other party hopes he will.

Believe me, I know. Because most guys are oriented toward beautiful—or at least pretty—and no matter how friendly they are, no matter how much they talk to me or flirt with me, they're not going home with me, and they're certainly not going to invite me to spend time with their little friend.

At least, not when they're sober. And I've been a bartender long enough to know, they're not worth a damn when they're drunk. After a while, you look for meaning, you know? Just a kind word, a phrase, a bit of understanding.

I try a little kindness once a night, just to keep my hand in the game, which was why I talked to Mr. Weird But Beautiful in the first place.

Sometimes kindness pans out. Sometimes it doesn't.

And sometimes it leads you places you never thought you'd go.

***

HE CAME BACK THE NEXT AFTERNOON. Mr. Weird But Beautiful, who never darkened my door on any day but Friday, had shown up on Saturday wearing a blue chambray shirt, faded jeans, shit-kickers with no added heel. If anything, he looked even more delectable. The blue shirt stretched just enough to show the muscles on his chest. The jeans hugged his ass the way...well, the way I wanted to.

He didn't sit at the bar. Instead, he took a table in the middle of the room.

And since none of the cocktail waitresses would go near him, I had to wait on him. From the bar, I said tiredly, "Beer and piña, right?"

He looked at me, those blue eyes flat, his expression reserved, his tone one you'd use with a six-year-old. "Just the beer."

So I brought him the light, still foaming over the stein, and onto the tray. Man, was I out of practice.

I set down the napkin, then the beer, and started to leave, when he said, "I've been thinking about our conversation."

"Good," I said, and returned the tray, wiping it down before I set it near the server's station.

"And I'd like to ask you a few questions," he said just a little louder.

Jodi, the cocktail waitress, raised a single eyebrow. It was her who-does-this-asshole-think-he-is? look.

But there was no one else in the place. So I told her to man the bar, and I walked back to him.

He kicked out the chair beside him. I sat. This wasn't going to be an easy conversation.

"So why doesn't it work?" he asked. "That line, as you call it."

My turn to give him the incredulous look, and I almost hauled out one of the sentences I'd been thinking since he first came in—"What? You were raised by wolves?"—but if I did, he'd bolt, and spend the rest of his life trying this stupid gambit at bars all over town, until he finally gave up and stayed home—alone—for the rest of his life.

I couldn't decide if that outcome was a crime against nature or just the way things should be.

For a minute, I toyed with answering the question delicately. But I'd tiptoed around delicate the day before, and it hadn't worked. This guy had spent *all night* wondering why "Say hello to my little friend," repelled women. He wasn't going to get delicate.

He might not even get blunt.

"Look," I said in my best I've-been-around-the-block voice, "we all know that most men name their penis, okay? We know you have a close relationship—a friendship—with that part. We just don't need to know it from the moment—"

"You think Marty is my penis? Are you nuts?" He stood up, bumped the table, and knocked over the stein. I slid my chair back so I wouldn't get doused in light beer.

Jodi tossed me the bar rag, but she wasn't getting anywhere near good ole WBB.

"Who else would he be?" I asked as I set the rag on the table and went for some bar napkins.

"My friend," WBB said. "You know, the guy who comes in here with me. The guy who drinks the piña coladas."

"I hate to tell you this, pal," I said as I tossed half the napkins on the table and the other half on the stain spreading across the floor. "But you come in here alone."

I expected an argument. I expected him to tell me all about this Marty, who accompanied him. I expected to hear every detail about the delusion.

Instead, WBB said, "That fucking son of a bitch," handed me a twenty, and walked out of the bar.

***

HE WALKED BACK IN AN HOUR LATER, dragging an ugly little man who had blood dripping from his nose. WBB picked up the little man—who couldn't have been more than three feet tall—and said,

"This. This is my little friend. Marty the fucking bastard. Say hello, Marty."

"Hello," the little man said in a nasal tone. He was dripping blood over the floors I had just cleaned the beer off of.

"Hello," I said. "Do you want to press charges? I can call the police."

The little man shook his head. Blood dripped everywhere.

"Show the nice lady what you can do, Marty," WBB said. "She's been kind to me. She deserves to know."

I flushed at the word "kind." No one had noticed before.

Marty closed his eyes. His nose was still dripping.

WBB shook him. "*Show* her."

And Marty disappeared. But the blood kept dripping on my floor. Ping, ping, ping.

Jodi and I exchanged glances. I'd seen a lot of strange things in my bar, but that was the first legitimate disappearing man.

"Now," WBB said. "Explain what was going on."

He shook his fists. Only Jodi and I knew that there was a little guy between them.

Either that or WBB was David Fucking Copperfield.

"*Tell* them," WBB said.

"We had a bet," the little guy said, and reappeared as he spoke. He was dangling between WBB's hands and looking as forlorn as a human being could. "We bet that no matter how good-looking he is, he couldn't get me a date."

"The rest of it," WBB said.

The little guy sighed.

WBB shook him again.

"We handicapped him," the little guy said, "by making him say, 'Say hello to my little friend.' You know, like in golf. Figuring the good player needed a level playing field with the ugly player. Me."

"Ugly." WBB said. "Damn straight."

I didn't say anything. I'd seen bar bets before. But judging from WBB's face the day he first came in—all stunned at the way the bar looked and smelled—he didn't. He had no idea that cheating was part of the process.

"How much was the bet for?" I asked.

"The year-end bonus," WBB said. "Five grand."

"He doesn't need his," the little guy said. "People give him stuff because he's so pretty."

I stared at WBB. His beautiful blue eyes flashed. He was furious.

He shook the little guy one more time for good measure. "Tell her the rest of it. I'd say, 'Say hello to my little friend.' And then you *what*?"

The little guy cleared his throat. "I disappeared."

He vanished then quickly reappeared.

"To everyone except me," WBB said. "I could see the little bastard."

"I hate to tell you this," I said, "but he disappeared long before you came into the bar. If he really was with you."

"He was," WBB said. "*Tell* her."

The little guy shrugged one imprisoned shoulder. The movement looked like it hurt. "It's my only talent.

It's all I can do. I trained it. Because people always looked at me with pity. I'm short and I'm ugly and you wouldn't believe the jokes."

"So you turned the table on your friend?" I asked. "A man who was going to help you? You played a trick on him?"

"He promised he wouldn't," WBB said. "He promised he'd stay visible."

"I did!" The little guy said.

"To me," WBB said. "And only me. The man who believed in him. I figured once someone talked to him, she'd want to go out with him. I used to think he was clever."

The little guy tried to wipe his nose but WBB held him fast.

"I *believed* in him," WBB said, and dropped him.

The little guy bounced in the pool of his own blood.

"Fucking bastard," WBB said, and left.

And of course, I never saw him again.

***

His little friend, on the other hand, haunts my bar like an out-of-work Rumplestiltskin. I think he makes his living by winning bar bets.

Like "betcha I can't appear and reappear." Like "I can make a piña colada vanish without even touching it." Like "I bet a handsome man like you can't get a woman to give me a second glance."

I let him stay. He's a curiosity. Now that they're used to him, the regulars place bets right alongside his. The entire place is getting rich.

Except me.

Because there's a part of me that still wants the fairy tale. You know, you help the gorgeous guy, and even though you're a plain Cinder Ella, he sees through the grime and makes you his princess.

But WBB hasn't come back. I haven't even gotten enough courage to ask his little friend for WBB's real name.

I know real life is not a fairy tale.

But I also know that tiny men who look like Rumplestiltskin can't disappear at will.

And yet this one does.

Somehow that's not quite enough to overcome my belief in the way the world really works.

You see, I own a bar. I know that people never change their orientation. And WBB, for all his willingness to help his little friend, was oriented toward beautiful—or at least pretty.

And no matter how nice I was, and how much I was willing to help him, and how much his pride made him come back to talk to me, to explain he really wasn't crazy, I knew he wasn't going home with me.

I knew he was never going to invite me to spend time with his little friend.

Victims

i

HER NAME HAD SHOWN UP twice before, in '68 when Nichols had run for governor of California, and in '72 when he made his unsuccessful bid for the presidency. No one had investigated her. Women's issues were different in those days, and women were not viewed as the voting block they are now. Besides, we couldn't make anything on Nichols stick.

We decided to investigate her before we talked with Senator Lurry. The task of interrogating her came to me.

I used Senator Lurry's outer office because it looked properly intimidating—mahogany trim, marble inlay floors. The desks were wide, oak and handmade. A coffeemaker, constantly in use, sat on top of one of the green metal filing cabinets, but the rich scent of French Roast couldn't overlay the mausoleum stench of an ancient building that has stood in humidity for a generation too long.

I arrived a half hour early, then adjusted my tie and peered at my reflection in the shiny glass on top of the secretary's desk. The cowlick had refused to be tamed again. I licked my hand and patted the spot, wishing for the fifteenth time that I could use boyish to my advantage. From the neck down I was perfect: broad shoulders tapering into narrow hips, legs firm and muscular. My face was the major problem. Oval-shaped with wide eyes and pouty lips, it made me look like a twelve year-old in his father's body, which was the reason I worked behind the scenes for Senator Lurry instead of out front as most of the Cattons had in the past.

I didn't dare look naive in front of a woman named Veronique.

Especially a woman with a history like hers.

Downstairs a door slammed shut. I jumped. High heels clicked on the marble floor, the sound echoing in the empty building. I had often worked late, but never alone. Near midnight on those evenings, the place had a hum to it that I always associated with an election or a smear campaign. Never with an interview.

She had insisted on the time. "A woman in my profession," she had said, her voice husky through the phone lines, "looks best after dark."

I tugged on my black suitcoat. I wasn't really alone. Morse sat in the Senator's office, watching through the fake mirror in case the lady decided to ply her trade on me.

The footsteps grew closer. I rearranged the papers on the desk top, toyed with sitting down, and then decided to remain standing. I still hadn't learned all the tricks to power and intimidation.

The door opened and she slipped in. She was heart-breakingly thin, with perfect legs that tapered into a model's body. She wore spike heels, fishnets, and a leath-er mini-skirt that revealed each curve around her hips. Her black Irish lace blouse set off her porcelain skin. Her lips were dark red, her cheekbones high and her eyes an amazing shade of brown. No wonder she ran the most exclusive escort service in D.C. No man would be able to say no to her.

I stepped from behind the desk, resisting the urge to wipe my hands on my pants legs. I approached her, palm extended. "Reese Catton."

She placed her fingers lightly in mine. Her skin was cool, not cold as I had expected. "Veronique de la Mer."

Her voice was husky and warm. A tingle ran up my spine. Ever since vampires and vampirism had come out of the closet five years ago, the news and the tabloid press had been full of articles on the sensual effect of the pred-ator-victim relationship. It didn't seem to matter that all but a few psychopathic vampires had long ago given up killing human prey—choosing instead to use a hand-ful of willing people to provide blood, much as a blood bank did for a hospital—("the supermarket approach to blood-sucking," the *New York Times* had called it)—the fear, loathing, and sexual tension caused by the human/ vampire relationship filled the popular imagination.

Just as she filled mine.

Dry facts weren't giving me control. I took a deep breath, and slid into the leather chair behind the desk.

"I hope you understand why we contacted you," I said.

"Oh, yes." Her voice was soft. "It's about Governor Nichols."

She had an edge when she spoke his name, a frisson of anger just beneath the surface. I swallowed, feeling calmer. "I hope you don't mind if I tape this conversation."

"I expected you to," she said, and folded her hands demurely on her lap. I pressed the button underneath the desk, activating the room's taping system, and wondered for a moment if vampires' voices taped. But I knew they did. We had gotten tape on one just a few weeks ago. They didn't reflect or film—but that was because of the silvering in the mirrors.

"I understand," I said, leaning forward and placing my arms on the desk, "that you've never spoken with anyone about Governor Nichols."

She smiled, revealing straight, white teeth. "Oh, I've spoken with people," she said. "Only no one believed me."

I froze. Her last sentence had thrown me. We were planning, with her cooperation, to smear the former governor by linking him to a vampire as her cow. Our preliminary surveys of 150 voters showed that such a thing would work as effectively as gay bashing had in the eighties. "What do you mean?"

"On July 4, 1966, your friend, the former governor of California, raped me." She never took her gaze off mine. She spoke calmly, but the ends to the words were clipped as if she had to spit them out.

I let out the air I had been holding. She was lying. We couldn't bring this to the media. They would skin her alive. "Why didn't you press charges?"

A half smile, curving those delicate lips into her firm cheekbones. "I tried. It was 1966. I was told that a woman who ran an escort service shouldn't complain when she got famous business."

"Who told you that?"

"The detective in charge," she said. "An unfortunately deceased man named Petrie. His superior officers backed up his prejudice. I haven't spoken of the incident since. I figure it would be even tougher to convince people now that they know I belong to a completely different race."

"Why didn't you go after him?"

Her eyes seemed to tilt downward with an expression of deep sadness, as if she were disappointed in me for asking the question. "Come now, Mr. Catton. What did you expect me to do? Fly into his house on bat wings and rip out his throat?"

"Something like that," I mumbled. My cheeks grew warm. I guess I had expected that. Old fictional images died hard. Studies had shown that vampires lacked the ability to shapeshift and mesmerize, although they did have centuries' long lifespan and the appearance of eternal youth.

"Mr. Catton, I have used my political contacts for the better part of two decades to keep the former Governor of California out of the presidency. But times are changing, and the country doesn't seem to care what kind of man he is as long as he presents a positive media image. Grandfatherly always seems to work in this country. Well, as you know, any connection with me would ruin Nichols' grandfatherly image." She stood and smoothed her skirt. "The problem you face is that I am unwilling to be linked to that slime romantically or parasitically. We will denounce him as a man capable of extreme violence or you will not have my cooperation."

"Forgive me," I said from my chair, "but I don't think Middle America would care that you got raped."

She took a step backwards as if I had slapped her myself. "I suppose you're right," she said. "Middle America would simply figure that a woman like me deserved it."

ii

I WAS SHAKING by the time I got home. Alison had gone to bed, leaving a single light on near the fireplace. Embers glowed, light reflecting across the shiny hardwood floor. This place always filled me with a kind of pride—the way the couches framed the oriental rugs, the fresh flowers on the Duncan Fife end tables, the lemon-scented neatness of the condo itself. Even though I had been raised a Catton, my mother kept a messy, "lived-in" house in Connecticut that hid my father's wealth. I preferred an immaculate, House Beautiful style.

Except tonight. Tonight I wanted to kick off my shoes, scrunch the rugs, and huddle near the television set. But

I pulled off my shoes and hung them on the shoe rack in the closet beside the door, walked stocking-footed across the slippery floor and sat at the dining room table, staring at the fruit basket, perfectly arranged, with bananas on the side, oranges at the base and apples on top.

Veronique had gotten to me.

I had never been naive, not even when I had come to Washington as a page for Senator Lurry fifteen years ago. Any pretensions I had may have had remaining toward Truth, Justice, and the American Way were then bled out of me in George Washington's poli sci department and at Harvard Law. Politics in this country had become the battle of the image. Whoever controlled the media controlled the campaign.

Veronique and her escort service hadn't been necessary in '68 and '72. Nichols had done a good job of destroying his own campaign. Then he disappeared behind the scenes, became a scion of the Republican party, helped Reagan and Bush achieve office, and maintained his own series of perks. The media had forgotten all about the bumbling "youth" candidate who had challenged Nixon in the '72 primaries, and saw only the trim, natty grandfather who had helped the Republicans become a power in the eighties. A viceless, happily married man who spoke of family values, and allowed Pat Robertson to fund his campaign.

The kind of man Senator Lurry—whose presidential ambitions had died the night of his daughter's suicide in '80—despised. Lurry had vowed to clear the way for the Democratic challenger, whether that might be Clinton, Gore, or a wildcard no one had ever heard of. We had demolished Quayle before he even announced, but Nichols was proving to be as Teflon as Reagan had been.

The rape charge wouldn't stand. I had been right. Middle America wouldn't tolerate it. They would bring down the messenger.

I sighed, and placed my forehead on my arms. We had contacted Veronique because the call girls had not so inexplicably shut up, the records had disappeared on the reported spousal abuse in the mid-seventies, and the college plagiarism charge hadn't caused a ripple in the polls. An affair with a vampire, we figured, still had taint, even though it was nearly thirty years old.

Although it would be a gamble. If word of the smear got out, Lurry would lose his position as champion of the non-traditional. Vampires, gays and minorities formed a large percentage of his constituency.

If Lurry got caught, he would, of course, blame his assistants.

He would blame me.

iii

"WHAT'D HE DO?" Lurry asked. "Force her to bite him at gunpoint?"

He was a big man who barely fit in the desk chair that had been specially designed for him ten years previously.

He had long jowls that spoke of too many meals and the red, bulbous nose of a hard-core alcoholic. His voice boomed, even in the small office. It always amazed me that he could tarnish the image of anyone.

I shot a glance at Stuckey, his press secretary. She had a small, heart-shaped face, almond eyes, and cafe au lait skin. Her mixed heritage was as much a part of her job as her way with words.

"She didn't go into the details of the rape," I said.

Stuckey leaned back in her chair, her long slender fingers playing with the ruby on her left hand. "We would need proof of some kind. Police report, photographs—"

"Photographs are impossible." I picked the lint off my black pinstriped pants leg. "And she said that the police refused to believe her."

"If they were called to the site, someone had to write it up," Stuckey said. "It's probably buried in some back file in a basement somewhere. I'll bet Nichols didn't think to cover his tracks on this one."

"I don't see any reason why he had to. Reese was right. Middle America isn't going to give a damn that some blood-sucking parasite got slapped around thirty years ago."

Stuckey jutted out her narrow chin. Forty years ago, someone might have said the same about her. I hated it when she got that look. "Be careful, Senator," she said. "The Republicans would love to hear you talking like that."

"For god's sake," he said, leaning forward. His exquisitely tailored suit strained at its buttons. "It's the truth."

"There's another truth," Stuckey said. "She has been an influential member of Washington Society since the thirties. She contributes to all sorts of charities, and it could be said that her escort business provides a necessary service for this community. There is no overt evidence of prostitution, and any employee who provides sexual services on a regular basis drops off the payroll of the service and appears on the payroll of the client. Would she make an articulate spokesman, Catton?"

I nodded. Something about Lurry's reaction was bothering me. "She would, except that we can't film her."

"That doesn't matter," Stuckey said. "Neither can they. I say let's see what we got and then make a decision. We might be able to use the woman after all."

"No," Lurry said. He folded his hands over his chest.

Stuckey raised one eyebrow. She opened her mouth to speak as I put a finger on her arm.

"What's your connection with her, Senator?" I asked.

His expression didn't change but his gaze seemed to go flat. It was a look I recognized from his press conferences: the Lurry Method of Avoiding the Truth. "She runs an escort service for the Washington elite, Reese. There's no telling what kind of dirt we might inadvertently dig up."

I suppressed a sigh. Lurry had always been a wild man; the wildness had gotten worse since his daughter's death. During my college years, the staff had worked hard at covering his destructive tracks all over this city. I had worked hard when I came on board the second time to hold onto other staff members, particularly the women, who hated his roving hands and not-so-subtle innuendo. The others trusted me, because they knew I was a family man, a man who would never treat others the way Lurry did.

But this was something that had fallen through the cracks.

Stuckey had come to the same conclusion. She hated working for Lurry, hated that the man behind the excellent political record was a petty tyrant, sexist and a bigot. "It might be your last chance to get Nichols," she said.

Lurry spun the swivel on his chair so that he looked out the window instead of staring at us. He was silent for a long time. Finally he said, "I don't care. We can't afford the risk. We'll have to find some other way."

"I doubt there is another way," Stuckey said. She left the room. I followed more slowly. As I closed the door, I saw Lurry reach into his liquor cabinet. It was too early to drink, even for him.

iv

DESPITE LURRY'S REFUSAL to pursue the investigation, Stuckey continued. So did I. I was too intrigued to let it go. Maybe after we had the evidence, Lurry would allow us to run to the media. It had happened before.

Stuckey put one of our best detectives on the case, a secret infiltrator who had no visible connections to us. The detective would make it look to the police like an investigation of Veronique de la Mer instead of an investigation of Nichols.

That would keep the information out of the press until we were ready to put it there ourselves.

Stuckey and I were supposed to meet with the Senator after the detective's report came in, but I had some questions of my own to answer.

Veronique's escort service had headquarters near the Hill. I parked a block away, and waited until no one was looking before I entered the building. The elevator took me to the sixth floor offices. As I stepped through the double glass doors, a level of tension left me.

The offices were tasteful. The colors were out of date: the muted grays and pinks of the mid-eighties, but the garish purples and neon greens of the early nineties would have looked out of place here. Flowers in Waterford crystal vases stood on runners that crossed antique tables. All of the furniture was antique, mixing periods to great effect: the tables were Early American, the couches late Victorian, the lighting and the crystal were modern. The decor gave the feel of a place that had been in business for a long, long time. The carpet absorbed my footfalls, and I was alone in the waiting room. I assumed that was on purpose. It made the clients feel as if discretion was part of the service.

A woman entered through a sliding glass door. She wore a white silk dress that flowed around her voluptuous body. Her long black hair flowed down her back, as untamed as the dress. "Do you have an appointment, sir?"

Her voice was as well modulated as the rest of her. A shiver ran down my spine. "No," I said, a little more harshly than I expected. "I am from Senator Lurry's office. I would like to see Veronique."

The woman nodded once. "Come with me," she said, and without waiting, went back through the glass doors.

The hallway was long and narrow, and smelled faintly of lilacs. Closed doors along each side gave this area a forbidding feeling that the front didn't have. Privacy above all else.

How odd. Veronique mastered privacy in her business, yet she was willing to give it all away to bring down Nichols.

She really had to hate him.

The woman opened the double mahogany doors at the end of the hallway, then stepped aside so that I could enter. I stepped into another waiting room, although this one was more flamboyant than the one I left. The colors were red, black and deep browns, and all of the furniture was late Edwardian: heavy with thick upholstery. The room had a masculine feel as if it were designed by a man for a woman.

The door closed behind me. I sat on the edge of the couch, feeling sixteen again, and at the interview for my page position. I tugged on the knees of my trousers. They were tight across the groin.

A door opened, and then Veronique was in the room. She wore her hair piled on top of her head, revealing a slender well-formed neck. This time she wore a suit. The jacket was open, and the shell was cut low across her breasts, revealing cleavage and a bit of nipple. She sat on the edge of her desk and crossed her legs. "I didn't expect to see you here, Mr. Catton."

I swallowed. I was a happily married man. Alison and I had a good sex life. I didn't need anything else. "I'm here on business."

She smiled. "Most people are."

"No," I said. "For Senator Lurry."

"Ah." She got off the desk and retreated behind it, tugging her coat across her chest. "You want to know details. How can a human male rape a woman of superior strength? It's really quite easy, Mr. Catton. It simply takes planning. He must learn where I sleep, for that's when I am most vulnerable, and learn how to tie me up, how to immobilize my mouth. Determination, Mr. Catton —"

"That's not why I'm here," I said. I couldn't stand the calm tone she was using with me. "I've been thinking about this. We're investigating your claim now, but it doesn't completely make sense to me. Assume that I believe you, what's in this for you? You have other, more subtle ways to bring down Nichols. Why choose a haphazard method that may not work?"

She smiled and leaned back, letting the coat pull open again. The shell was thin and it stretched across her chest, outlining her breasts in detail. Her nipples were hard points against the material.

I forced myself to look at her eyes.

"You're very smart, Mr. Catton," she said.

I licked my lips. She made me nervous, here, in her lair. "I try to be."

"Then perhaps you will understand that I am tired of being hidden. My people have been out of the closet, to use your quaint phrase, for five years now, and we are still fighting myths and prejudices. We live long lives, and have experiences that encompass entire generations. We understand policy and its ramifications better than you do. But our limitations, Mr. Catton, became obvious once the camera was invented. We cannot run for office. We could not even try until a few years ago."

I tugged again at my pants legs. It was good they couldn't run, good that television cameras couldn't pick them up. With their charisma, they would win, every time. "People are too afraid of you to elect you."

"Yes," she said. "I know. But things change over time. We have seen that with African Americans and with women. We have decided that it is better to fight in an open forum than behind the scenes."

"To put you up against Nichols' media machine is to sacrifice you to the prejudices of the American people. You'll lose."

"Perhaps," she said. "But I'll damage Nichols, and I'll start the awareness that vampires are not the all evil, all powerful beings the movies have made them out to be."

I ran a hand along the crushed velvet upholstery. "I don't understand how choosing to become a victim will help you politically."

She shrugged, and smiled, just a little. "Then, Mr. Catton, you're not as smart as I thought."

v

I IMMEDIATELY HURRIED HOME. Fortunately Alison was there. Much to her surprise, I dragged her to bed, and we made love like newlyweds in their sexual prime. We had just finished when the doorbell rang.

She brushed the hair from her forehead. "You go on," she said, pushing me a little. "I need to shower. I'm already late for a Women in Business meeting."

I slid on a pair of jeans, walked barefoot to the door, and looked through the peephole. Stuckey was there, her face pale beneath the make-up. She clutched a stack of folders to her chest. Her briefcase rested on the floor beside her.

I pulled the door open.

"We need to talk," she said, and came in without an invitation. Her shoes left little prints on the hardwood floor. She set everything on the dining room table, pushing the basket of fruit aside to make room.

I sat down beside her, opened the files, and barely looked up when Alison kissed me good-bye. The files were dusty, the old police reports more detailed than I had expected, as if someone had been planning a case. A client had found Veronique, naked, blood-covered, and half dead in her waiting room. She had been tied with silver wire, a garlic bulb shoved in her mouth, and slashed from groin to sternum with a knife. The reports were filed by four separate officers, and a pathologist. Veronique had been conscious enough to demand her private doctor, and instead of being treated by the hospital staff, she had been treated by a man now known as the vampire's equivalent of doctor to the stars.

The files included photos of the crime scene, and Veronique's account, both on tape, and in writing, of the rape itself. The investigation ended as soon as the nature of Veronique's profession became known.

Stuckey watched me as I read Veronique's account. Nichols had not been alone. Four other politicians of his generation had been there to take care of Veronique properly. Three of the four were dead—one in a single engine plane crash over the Appalachians, one in an unsolved murder in Mexico, and one of an undiagnosed variety of pernicious anemia which the doctor associated with leukemia but which was now known to be caused by a bad reaction to secretions in vampire saliva.

The fourth was alive: Senator Jason Lurry, then a first-term Congressman from the great state of Texas.

I brought my head up. Stuckey was watching me, elbow on the table, chin resting on her palm. "She set us up," I said.

Stuckey rolled her eyes. "Veronique is not the problem," she said. "It's Lurry. He lied to us and to his constituents from the beginning. Did you read why he participated?"

I shook my head. I had stopped when I saw his name.

"Because she was withholding favors from them. *Political* favors. She was refusing to use her sexual influence to aid their careers."

I let my breath out slowly. "Raping her was certainly not the way to get her to help."

"No," Stuckey said, "but it sent a message throughout the community. A lot of people knew what she was. They must have figured these men had a lot of muscle behind them to get her as badly as they did."

I rubbed the bridge of my nose. A headache was building behind my eyes. It all made sense now. Lurry and Nichols had ceased being friends in '67. Something must have come between them then, something to do with Veronique. They managed to succeed without her, but not to the heights they had wanted. And whenever they had come close to achieving those heights, something had successfully damaged their careers—like Lurry's daughter's suicide.

"What I don't understand is why she's doing this now," I said. "I talked to her. I said going public would make her a victim, and why would anyone want to be a victim? She laughed at me and called me naive."

Stuckey blinked at me, and then grinned. "You're not naive," she said. "You're just privileged. Reese Catton, son of politicians, product of private schools and Ivy League law schools. Even your name has the sound of wealth."

I squirmed, suddenly cold without my shirt. "What the hell does that mean?"

"It means you're one of the lucky few who've never been victimized." She leaned forward, a flush rising beneath her dusky skin. "Reese, honey, victims are victims when they remain quiet. They gain power when they speak out."

The headache had moved to my temples. "She had power. It looks like she controlled their careers from the inside."

"But that's a revenge cycle," Stuckey said, "and no more empowering than punching a man who mugged you. You need to read more about ways to help the powerless. Look what empathy did for Bobby Kennedy."

"Yeah," I said, standing. "It got him assassinated."

vi

THIS TIME WE MET in neutral territory, at the Lincoln Memorial. I waited on the steps after dark, in the shadow of Honest Abe himself.

Honest Abe, who had suspended civil rights, and freed the slaves as a matter of political expediency. Honest Abe, who really wanted to send all the blacks back to Africa.

I heard her before I saw her. Heels clicking against the sidewalk, a purse clutched to her arm. She wasn't wearing hooker clothes or a business suit. This time, she wore jeans and a mohair sweater. The outfit suited her more than the others had.

"You set me up," I said, before I could see her face in the streetlight.

"No." She climbed the stairs and sat beside me on the top. She smelled faintly of lilacs. "I have just learned that it is easier to convince people when they discover the information for themselves. You wouldn't have believed me if I attacked your precious senator. You believe me now."

I did that. If nothing else, I believed Veronique's version of those events back in 1966. "What do you want from me?"

"We need a spokesman. You are our best choice. You are young, moving into that youthful handsomeness that this country associates with its romantic leaders. But the problem is you have no dreams, no ideals. We will give those to you." She ran a hand through her hair. There was nothing seductive about her this night. "You see, what your histories have forgotten is that the symbiosis went beyond the physical. Your people provided the energy, the power, and the drive. Ours the sense of community and continuity. Over the centuries, we failed to keep our end. We stagnated, and you rebelled—a rebellion that culminated with the invention of the camera and became codified with the publication of Stoker's horrible political tract. But we have learned our lesson. We would like to forge a new voice in the political history of the western world. We would like a new alliance, and we need your help."

I leaned back, resting my elbows on the cool concrete stairs. I should have been used to power games;

I had initiated enough myself. But I had been off balance in this one from the beginning. "Why me? Why not someone like Stuckey?"

"Because," she said, "you have no personal axes to grind, no commitment to anything except yourself, your lovely wife, and your home. We don't want someone with other ties that might interfere with our cause."

Words were carved into the walls above me. Great words, spoken by a man considered by many to be one of our best leaders. Who knew why he ran for office. Power-madness? A belief he could make a difference? Ego? All three or none of the above?

I shook my head. "I'm sorry," I said. "I don't know anything about you people. For all I know, you could be trying to take over the country."

She smiled, her teeth flashing in the streetlights. "Isn't that what every special interest group hopes to do?"

"Not every special interest group has the power of persuasion that you people have."

She touched my hand. Her fingers were cold. "I should make myself clear. I'm not asking you to run for President. I want you to resign as Lurry's aide, then help me make a public case against them."

Her fingers were long and slender, the nails tapered. "Forgive me," I said, keeping my voice soft. "But I was right that first night. Middle America won't care that you were raped."

"Make them care. That would be your job."

I moved my arm out of her grasp. "There are better people for that. Image brokers, people who make their living changing public opinion."

"But none are as unimpeachable as you." She leaned back beside me. "Think of it. You worked for Senator Lurry. You discovered the information yourself. It so appalled you that you are jeopardizing your own political career to speak out against him."

I tilted my head back so that I couldn't see her. Abe's carved legs, spread slightly apart, towered above me. She would do this, with or without me. And she would fail, but the die would be cast. Conversations would start; people would talk; ideas would get aired like they had at the beginning of each intellectual and perceptual revolution.

The balance of power was shifting beneath me. I could cling to the old or leap to the new. Or I could attempt to straddle the middle, and watch the world as I knew it crumble beneath my feet.

I had planned to resign anyway.

I needed a new job.

"Let me bring Stuckey along and I'll do it," I said.

"You may have anyone you want on your team." Veronique stood and wiped off the back of her jeans. "Come to me after you've publicly announced your resignation. We'll finalize our agreement then."

She walked down the steps, heels clicking until the darkness swallowed her. I didn't know how I ever thought she wanted to be a victim. She had more power than all the rest of us combined—the power of her convictions. I envied that. It was something I had never seen in Washington.

Maybe the world was shifting more than I thought.

About the Author

AWARD-WINNING, BESTSELLING WRITER Kristine Kathryn Rusch has published books under many names and in many genres. Her vampire novel, *Sins of the Blood*, has a cult following worldwide. Her fantasy novels about the Fey have been published all over the world, and were recently rereleased in the United States as audio books by Audible.com. They will be reissued in print in 2013 by WMG Publishing. She has won the World Fantasy Award and is the former editor of *The Magazine of Fantasy & Science Fiction*. She also writes fantasy novels under the name Kristine Grayson. For more information on her work, go to www.kristinekathrynrusch.com.

Also by
Kristine Kathryn Rusch

The Fey Series:

Destiny (A Short Novel)
Sacrifice
Changeling
The Rival
The Resistance
Victory
Black Queen
Black King

Standalone Fantasy Novels:

The White Mists of Power
Heart Readers
Traitors

WMG
Publishing